THE TACHARAN

A Story of Loch Ness

Keith D. Graham

Loch Ness Facts:

22 Sq. Miles of freshwater – largest body of water in the United Kingdom by volume. Contains almost double the amount of water compared to all the lakes in England and Wales combined.

Average temp: 5 degrees Celsius (41 degrees Fahrenheit)

9 miles east-southeast of Inverness

Deepest point: Keith's Abyss approximately 889 ft. Discovered in 2016.

Virtually impossible to properly explore due to high concentrations of peat and sediment causing low visibility in the waters............

DEDICATION

I have quite a few people to thank for helping me make this dream a reality. First the two most amazing women on earth. My wife Leila Graham and my mom Marlene Fink. Thank you both for your love and your support. I wouldn't be where I am without the two of you.

Thanks to all my friends who reviewed my story and critiqued, made suggestions, and urged me along. Special thanks to Aubrey Peel for her challenging me to think harder.

Thanks to Goody Haines and Gary Fuller for my own private performance of The Parting Glass!

Gratitude to all the explorers and believers who keep Nessie alive. I know she's there and I look forward to meeting her one day!

Slainte Mhath,

Keith D. Graham

To My Readers:

Thank you for reading and supporting my work!

There are a few "Easter eggs" hidden in this story. I'm a big fan of Star Trek and Star Wars (yes you can like both). See if you can find them! Also look for Doctor Who eggs and there is one for fans of WWE Wrestling as well. Who knows? There may be more!

If you do find any, email me and let me know!

thetacharan@gmail.com

If you have any questions about the story, email me and I'll get back with you. I'd also love to hear your thoughts on my book and if you would like a sequel.

Happy Reading,

Keith D. Graham

CHAPTER ONE

Earth Year 1575

On certain fall nights, just before the cold winter, the fog is the thickest on Loch Ness. It moves across the waters and onto the land. So thick you could almost hold it in your hands, it hides everything, and that's when they come.

(Loch Ness is a perfect substitute for my people. We are the Tacharan. We came to Earth for sanctuary, for safety, for the preservation of our race.

Our name in the Old Gaelic means, "Changeling", "The ones left behind by fairies." Quite accidental, but suiting. Our home planet was almost wiped out by the Raiders. They scour the galaxies killing whole planets of peoples and then stealing the natural resources; water, minerals, food supplies, etc. They abused and destroyed their own planet, so they have no issues taking from others.

Luckily, they didn't completely eradicate us. A remnant of us remained and survived, but our water was virtually gone which destroyed our breeding pits. We needed to find another place to raise our young or the Tacharan would be a footnote in galactic history.

My people by nature are kind and benevolent. Our young are born under water where they must remain for 1 cycle (approximately 1 Earth year), and as they mature, they can breathe under water or surface air. The very young are quite vulnerable, without defense. They must be hidden from predators and are protected by a guardian assigned by our Chief Elder, Kem-ka-Jen.

We searched throughout the cosmos, sending our few remaining scout ships everywhere looking for an ideal planet. We found Earth. More specifically we found Loch Ness. Deep protected trenches, perfect temperatures, an abundant food supply, and most important, far from the territory of our enemies.)

Jal-sa-Lem – (So, I was the first Tacharan scout to visit the Sol System in the Earth year 1560. Well, that's not technically true. I'm the first scout to actually land on Earth, interact with a human, and find the ideal place for our needs. Our first scout found Earth in the year 565. His name was Jol-sa-Pel. His mission wasn't to find new breeding pits; we hadn't been attacked yet. No, his mission was completely exploratory and benign. Stories were circulated that he attacked and killed a man on the shores of Loch Ness, but this isn't true. We are peaceful beings. Anyway, back to my story.)

"Jal-sa-Lem to Central Command. I'm entering the Sol System now. The outer planets lack water and are too cold for our use. I'm checking the inner planets and then calling it." "Central Command to scout ship **Vanir**, while we appreciate that you have been out searching for quite some time, you cannot fail in this mission. Continue your search until you find new breeding pits. None of the other scouts have found anything

3

suitable, and two scouts have failed to report in. We fear the Raiders have caught them and knowing the Raiders, executed them. Our resources are in short supply and we cannot afford to search much longer. If you are not successful we fear for our future." Jal-sa-Lem hung his head at the news of his lost comrades. With determination, he swore, "I will not fail! Our children will live on! The Tacharan will NOT die away due to my failure!"

McDougal, Sean, and Fergus were doing what young men did best. Having spent the day working in the hemp fields, they were blowing off steam in McCallum's Tavern near the coast of Loch Ness. Sean and Fergus were twins, just turned 18. Ruddy complexion, lots of freckles, and skinny as willow sticks. Their family had recently come to Inverness after leaving Ireland. The Irish drought that had started in May of this year still didn't show signs of ending. McDougal on the other hand had lived here his whole 34 years of life. Standing six feet tall, he had shoulder length curly red hair and was clean shaven. Quite muscular from working on a farm his whole life he never seemed to lose the fights he often started.

David McCallum was a big man with a bigger smile. Standing six feet seven inches tall, he had owned and operated his tavern since before McDougal had been born. McDougal's parents had been friends of his before their deaths. McDougal's father passed away while being held prisoner in Newcastle Upon Tyne after the Battle of Solway Moss in November 1542. His mother died in 1558 due to smallpox. Truth be told, after his father's death, McDougal's mother was never the same. The light in her eyes died long before the smallpox took her. Despite a number of attempts on David's part, McDougal never got close to anyone after their deaths. That was why McCallum gave the trio some leeway in their tomfoolery. But even he could only handle so much. He normally lost his cool right about closing time when McDougal could more often than not, be counted on for breaking something.

'CRASH!'

"McDougal! I swear! If that chair is broken I'm gonna tear yer hide right off yer bones!" Boomed McCallum.

"No Sir!" Shouted McDougal. "Just knocked it over! Cracked my head on the floor tho!"

"I don't care aboot yer head boy! Time for you and yours to get out anyway. Go home fellas, its late."

Just then a local boy, William, came bursting in the tavern.

"Adhar Inneal! Adhar Inneal!" He yelled. "Someone come!"

The few remaining patrons started laughing at the boy. McCallum came over to shoo William out the door.

"Look here boy. Number one, it is way too late for you to be up and around, and number two, I don't allow fairy tales and boogeyman in my establishment. Now be off with you. McDougal! Walk this boy home so nothing happens to him."

"Seriously? Why me?" Asked McDougal.

"Because I said so and if you don't, I'll finish the head cracking the floor started on you! You need to grow up boy, get some purpose in your life. Just look at yerself. At yer age you should be married and have a few bairns of yer own running aboot. Instead yer hanging out here drinking yer wages away and living in me stables. Your parents would have wanted better for ya than just picking crops and drinking. Now get out of here!" Ordered McCallum.

McDougal said goodnight to Sean and Fergus and grabbing William by the arm, he headed out into the night. William kept babbling to him, but McDougal was paying him no mind.

When they reached Williams home McDougal was all for leaving quickly, but William stopped him.

"Please listen to me! I'm not making up a story! I truly did see something flying over Loch Ness! It was bright as a candle in spots and made a sound like nothing I've ever heard. Tell me you'll go take a look. Please?" Begged William.

"Fine boy. I'll go look around. But I'll be back tomorrow to smack you upside the head and tell you that I don't appreciate yer story!" Said McDougal. "Now get yerself to bed!"

McDougal soon found himself walking about the Loch searching for what he did not know. He wasn't afraid of being out in the night alone, though Williams story was a little off putting if he were honest with himself.

"Adhar Inneal!" (Sky machine in Gaelic) "Ridiculous!" said McDougal. "The bairn is crazy I tell ya! Great, now you're talking to yerself McDougal. Maybe you're the crazy one." "Still, young William swears by everything that's holy that he saw an Inneal in the sky over Ness. But carts don't fly!" he exclaimed. "The boy is either daft or pulling my leg. Either way, I'm freezing my arse off walking around the loch. One more shot of whisky and I'm headed home."

8

Just then, as he took a sip from his flask, he heard movement at the water's edge. 'Now what can that be?' he thought. 'Sounds like a lad and lass rolling around in the shallows!' As he came through the trees, he thought he had lost his mind. "What in God's name is this abomination?" he exclaimed as he crossed himself repeatedly.

In front of him, lying on the shore and tangled up in fishing nets, was the strangest creature he had ever seen. Half man half monster was the only thing he could think of. Maybe it was a fairy changeling, or a demon possessed man? Either way he was set to dispose of it! Its skin was a pale grey, mottled with black patches, no hair to be seen anywhere. Its head was armored with blue-green eyes, body well-muscled. If it were standing up it would probably be at least seven feet tall! Human shaped hands and feet, but with the snout of a dragon. Drawing his short sword, he advanced on the creature.

(Please!) He heard. (Don't harm me! I need your help.) McDougal lowered his sword and rubbed

9

his eyes. "I know its mouth didn't move, but I heard it speak!"

(You can hear my thoughts, and I can hear yours. Please, I am a friend and I need your help. Release me from this entanglement and I'll explain it all to you.)

"I think not you monster! You can stay tangled up and be happy you're not dead yet."

(I understand your trepidations McDougal, don't release me until you are convinced I will not harm you.)

 (How do ye know my name beast?!)

(I told you, I can read your thoughts, that's how we are communicating now. Without knowing my language, you can understand my thought processes. Thought is just a mathematical formula understood by all races. You haven't uttered a word since your first sentence to me, or didn't you notice?)

(Good Lord beast! You are right! This is witchcraft!)

10

(No McDougal, let me explain. My name is Jal-ka-Lem. My people are called the Tacharan in your language.)

(Changeling?) McDougal thought.

(Yes, very fitting McDougal, for my people do change. The form you see me in is our final transformation. Our new born are aquatic and must breathe underwater for one of your years. The majority of our people are much larger and can live either in water or on land, while the leaders of my people look as I do. We go through a radical renewal and become what you now see.)

(Incredible!) Said McDougal. (So, why are you here? Do you mean to take over our lands and destroy us? If that's your plan, I'll tell ya now, we Scots don't go peacefully!)

(No, we are not the Raiders, they are the ones who forced me here.)

Jal-sa-Lem proceeded to explain to McDougal what had happened to his planet and to the Tacharan.

(Those evil buggers!) McDougal exploded. (If I could, I would slaughter the lot of them for you!)

(While your sentiment is appreciated, that isn't our way my friend. However, if you are willing, we could use your help.)

(I may still be daft, but tell me what you need of me.)

(First, would you please let me loose of these bindings? I'm afraid they are cutting off my circulation!)

McDougal made quick work of the nets while Jal-sa-Lem explained his need.

(We will use Loch Ness to breed our young since the Raiders destroyed our breeding pits. When they are ready to birth, our females will come to Loch Ness. Once the young are born, the females will return to our planet and leave the young behind. Just a few at a time will be here along with a guardian to help them develop and keep them safe. My people are quite long lived, so we only breed a few young every couple of years. We can die by accident or intent, but for the most part we are immortal. When the children are ready, they will return home.)

(In your flying machine?) Asked McDougal.

(No!) Laughed Jal-sa-Lem. (My ship, the *Vanir*, is much too small for our young or our second phase adults to fit in. Plus, they don't have the dexterity to fly a ship either. No, I will be installing a transportation tunnel in the large trench under the water here. The tunnel will connect our worlds though space.)

(So, what do you need me for?) Asked McDougal. (Seems like you've gotten it well enough taken care of.)

(You will be our ally here on Earth and help hide us from your people and our enemies.)

McDougal thought for a moment. He said to himself, 'What's keeping me here? I have no family. My ma is gone, I never knew my father. I have no purpose in life just like McCallum said. Maybe this is what I'm supposed to be doing.'

13

Nodding his head and squaring his shoulders, McDougal knelt in front of Jal-sa-Lem and proclaimed, (I swear to protect your bairns and your secret unto my dying days.)

(My friend,) said Jal-sa-Lem, (you will be too important to our people to let you die. As I told you, my people are immortals and for your service to my race, so shall you be. Throughout time, you will need to move about, change names, and lie about your past so others don't discover the truth about you.)

McDougal laughed, (Sounds like fun!)

Installing the transportation tunnel and readying the trench took an earth month. Jal-sa-Lem and McDougal were careful to operate during the night's darkness to keep anyone from seeing them.

Once the tunnel was ready, the first transport took place. It was to bring Mar-wa-Len to Loch Ness. She would be the guardian for the Tacharan young on Earth.

(McDougal. Come to our meeting place please.) Thought Jal-sa-Lem.

(On my way!) Replied McDougal.

Upon his arrival, McDougal found not only Jal-sa-Lem, but another creature far different than what he expected.

"What is that!" exclaimed McDougal.

Standing in front of McDougal was not only his friend Jal-sa-Lem, but what only could be described in McDougal's mind as a monster of legends. Easily over 100 feet tall and probably longer from head to the powerful looking tail. Dark grey in color, smooth skinned, and piercing green eyes.

(Easy please my friend) thought Jal-sa-Lem. (Remember I told you about my people and how we transform over time. This is Mar-wa-Len. She is a member of our Space Services, our protectors. She is in our first transformation, or second form. She shall be the guardian.)

(My apologies Mar-wa-Len. I don't mean to offend ye. Just I never saw such a large beastie in me life! Yer aboot as big as me cottage!)

(No harm is done McDougal.) Replied Mar-wa-Len. (I understand the shock at seeing a new lifeform for the first time. Quite frankly your appearance startled me a bit too.)

(So tell me) Asked McDougal, (What do the bairns look like? Are they gonna shock me as well?)

Jal-sa-Lem chuckled. (Doubtful friend. They are much like Mar-wa-Len but much much smaller. Now, let us put this misunderstanding behind us and begin our work together.)

(Sounds good. What's our next step?) Thought McDougal.

Jal-sa-Lem answered, (First we will take you through the transformation process. I have the necessary equipment aboard my flier and Mar-wa-Len has brought the compounds we need from our home world.)

Aboard the Tacharan ship, McDougal was in shock.

"It's so bright! And white! And what are all those sounds? I know you told me aboot this machine of yours, but me head is swimming around! I think I'll be sick! McDougal exclaimed.

(Slow down my friend.) Thought Jal-sa-Lem. (I know this is a lot for you to take in. Hearing about something isn't the same as seeing. Sit here and relax.)

"Relax you say? I'll relax better after this." McDougal said taking a flask of whisky off his belt.

(Go easy on that.) Warned Mar-wa-Len. (The alcohol can impede the effects of our treatment.)

"So instead of being immortal I'll only live a thousand years? That's a risk I'm willing to take." Announced McDougal as he took a healthy swig.

Jal-sa-Lem chuckled. (I don't think we have any worries Mar-wa-Len. Whisky is to McDougal what water is to us!)

17

(You have much to teach me about humans McDougal.) Thought Mar-wa-Len. (I look forward to our conversations.)

"I as well." Said McDougal. "So tell me agin. What's gonna happen with this transformation?"

(Well.) Thought Jal-sa-Lem. (First you will enter a chamber that I can best describe to you as a bed of sorts, a sleeping pod. We will introduce a series of chemicals over a three-day period, during which you will be asleep. Biological changes will occur at your deepest cellular levels enabling you to live indefinitely. You will not show signs of aging however any wounds you suffer will remain with you. You will also not be able to reproduce due to the radioactive elements we are utilizing. Out worldly, no one will notice any changes.)

McDougal laughed, "I don't care how many times you explain this. I still don't understand most of what you said! I like the part aboot the three-day sleep though! One question though. Can ye make me taller?" he joked.

Mar-wa-Len answered. (We cannot do that, however, we could make you shorter. It is quite a simple procedure where we remove a portion of the bones in your legs…)

"Enough Enough!" said McDougal. "I was fooling around with ye! You're not to cut anything out of me. Is that understood?"

Jal-sa-Lem replied, (Easy friend. I don't believe Mar-wa-Len understood your humor. We won't do any such thing to you I promise.)

"All right then, I'm ready." Said McDougal.

"Transform me!"

So began the relationship between the Tacharan and humans. From time to time, the Tacharan provided McDougal with funds to help in his work. It's amazing that no matter when or where, a little gold in your pocket can help you forget seeing a monster in your loch. Other times, a few rounds of whisky and a pint or two can help distract attention to the other end of the loch far away from our alien bairns.

CHAPTER TWO

Earth Year 1577

Communique

From: Supreme Commander Rangellian

To: Captain SlayThan of the Battle Cruiser Lagartheria

"Your failure is unacceptable! While those creatures are still alive your life is in danger. We took the resources from their planet generations ago, how am I still hearing reports of their existence? Now find them, wipe them out or face your own execution!"

Captain SlayThan was angry. "Get me water!" he demanded. His steward asked him about his credit chip for the water. The captain yelled, "I'm the captain of this damn ship! If I want a cup of water, I get it! Now get out of here before I kill you!"

The steward ran out the door, knowing full well that Captain SlayThan could kill him quite easily. After all, he became the captains' steward after SlayThan killed his last one. The captains' foul mood was understandable. It had been his responsibility to wipe out the Tacharan home planet and while he had been almost completely successful, there was still a remnant of those vile beasts still living and for some reason, still producing offspring! The rumors and whispers throughout the system about how the Tacharan had outwitted the Raiders was giving false hope to some and misplace bravado to others. The Raiders trade partners were becoming increasingly bold in their dealings, and the council members were not happy at all. He thought to himself, "How are they doing this? Their breeding pits are completely destroyed, the water is gone, there is no way they should be having more children!" He must solve this problem; his people were not the forgiving kind.

"Helmsman, let's try this again! How many planetary systems have we searched in the past one and a half cycles?"

"That would be fifteen Sir."

"And how many more are within Tacharan scout ship and transportation tunnel capabilities?"

"Four Sir, with another twelve just outside safety protocol limits for their technology."

"Sciences, be useful! Best guess of the four remaining. Any intel on them, any insight you can give to save your job and your life?"

Science officer KaMal answered, "Of the four, the Orleath system would offer the best protection and resources for breeding. However, that system is in the opposite direction of the other three systems, and far removed from the other twelve Helmsman Ry-Lei mentioned."

The captain said, "Show me the systems on the viewer."

KaMal projected the display for the captain. "As you can see sir, Orleath is quite some distance, but again, it is the most likely scenario."

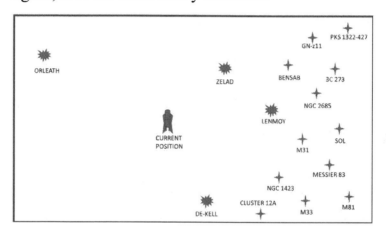

The captain drummed his fingers on his armrest. He thought, 'If I'm right, it's a council seat for me, but if I'm wrong, well, that's it.' He studied the display for another moment, and then said, "Helmsman, take us to the Orleath system, best possible speed!"

"Yes Sir!" Said Ry-Lei.

KaMal couldn't help but smile as he turned back to his station. 'Hopefully' he thought, 'I will finally be named the captain of this ship!'

CHAPTER THREE

Earth Year 1630

(Well my friend) thought McDougal, (you and I have done a fine job protecting the bairns from harm, haven't we?)

(Yes), replied Mar-wa-Len the guardian of the Tacharan young.   (Jal-sa-Lem was right in enlisting your help. We could not ask for a better ally than you McDougal.)

(Thank you, but I think it is time for McDougal to retire. The others are suspicious of my age even though I try to disguise the fact that I am not growing older.)

(I understand McDougal, and I have a thought. Across the highlands, there was a skirmish recently, and there are quite a few dead bodies. Perhaps you could retrieve one and burn down your home with the body inside? Everyone will assume it was you.)

(A bit gruesome, but aye, it would work.) Said McDougal. (I'd best get to it. But before I go, I've been thinking. Why don't we fix yer planet?)

(Fix it? We have some of our best minds working on that as we speak. In fact, one of our most brilliant educators and scientists, Cre-na-Tal, has dedicated her life to this. How do you propose we do it?)

(Why can't we send the water and fish from Loch Ness thru yer transport tunnel, and then send plants?)

(That's a bold plan my friend, but there's a few problems with this idea. First, all that water disappearing will draw attention. Second, the tunnel will not handle that kind of power drain. Additionally, our soil was stripped of all chemicals to support life. And even if we could overcome these challenges, we would end up with another planet in the Raiders space for them to plunder.

No my friend, this is a great thought, but it is not feasible.)

(Well I'm not giving up on this.) Said McDougal. (We will figure out a solution!)

(So where will you move and what shall I call you the next time we meet?)

(There's a small village south of here called Errogie that's about to have a visitor named Douglas.)

(Douglas? Humph. Kind of simple sounding! I like McDougal better.) Thought Mar-sa-Len.

(Douglas was my da's name, so I'll thank ye not to slander it!)

(No offense meant my friend. I'm still not used to how simple your names sound. Ours have such structure and yours seem so random.)

(None taken. Ours are structured too, maybe just not at the complexity of yours. We'll discuss it another time. Now I'm off to find my dead body!)

Said McDougal.   (Until we meet again, slainte mhath!)

CHAPTER FOUR

Earth Year 1578

"Warning! Warning! Imminent hull breach detected! Warning!" blared the robotic computer voice.

"Shut that damn blasted computer off before I kill someone!" shouted Captain SlayThan. "I can't hear myself think!"

"Yes Sir!" said Helmsman Ry-Lei as he struggled to control the ship and stay in his seat.

"What is happening?!" said SlayThan.

Science Officer KaMal said "Sir, we were struck by a cosmic cyclone and pushed into an asteroid belt. We are being assaulted on two fronts, electrical and physical. I believe the ship will suffer a catastrophic failure soon."

"Raise our protective fields and get us out of here!" screamed SlayThan.

"Protective fields are inoperable Sir." Replied Ry-Lei.

"Well what is working on this ship?" asked the captain.

"Actually, in addition to the field failure, we are losing life systems, gravity plating, transportation, lighting, and several non-essential systems." Stated KaMal.

"I asked what IS working, not what is failing KaMal!"

"In that case Sir, the only system which does not show any significant loss is our weapons banks. They are fully functional."

The captain bellowed, "Then fire all weapons!"

"At what Sir?" said Ry-Lei. "You can't shoot a cyclone and as for the asteroids, the targeting systems….."

"I know." Said the captain. "Targeting systems are offline. I get the picture. What happened KaMal? You said this was the best system to find the Tacharan!"

"Yes Sir, none of our scans showed this cosmic cyclone and as for the asteroid field, I believe it is a recent development from an exploded moon nearby. None of this was predictable."

"You are very calm for someone who is about to die KaMal!"

"Death comes to all captain. It only matters how we face it."

"Warning! Hull breach detected! Decks 7, 8, 9, and 10. Venting environment and debris."

"On viewer." Said SlayThan.

On the screen, they could see the vast gash in the side of their cruiser. "Magnify." Said the captain.

As they watched, they could see the cloud of atmosphere leaking out of the wounded vessel along with furniture, equipment, and bodies.

"Debris says the computer. Our comrades are nothing but trash to this stupid machine!" swore Ry-Lei.

"The computer is correct." Stated the captain. "As of now, that is just what they are. They can't help us survive this mess, so they are as useless as yesterday's garbage. Just like this lump of flesh lying at my feet."

Ry-Lei looked down at the captain's former steward. His neck had been broken in one of the first asteroid strikes to the ship.

"Captain." Said KaMal. "I believe we can land on the planet's surface. It won't be gentle, but we will make it."

"And then be stuck here for gods know how long?! No! Get us out of here!" yelled SlayThan.

"Not possible Sir," said Ry-Lei. "We either land or be destroyed in this field."

"I concur captain." Said KaMal. "Landing and waiting for rescue is our only option."

"For you two, and whatever's left of the crew, it is. For me, landing is a death sentence if I can't bring my ship home! Now again, get us out of here!"

"That isn't happening SlayThan." Stated KaMal. "For what it's worth, this is now my ship and crew. You have terrorized them long enough." And with that, KaMal drew a tazze pistol and stunned SlayThan unconscious.

"Ry-Lei, see if you can get some crew up here to help land the ship. Oh, and a couple of security crew to escort the 'captain' to the holding cells. I'm sure the Supreme Commander will want him returned to the home ships in good condition for his trial. Once we land, send a distress signal to the fleet signed; Acting Captain KaMal."

"Aye Captain!" said Ry-Lei. "Congratulations Sir!"

CHAPTER FIVE

Earth Year 1634

"Douglas! Suppers ready! Come in to eat!" yelled Elspeth, the seven-year-old daughter of McKenzie.

Douglas put down his gardening tools, walked over to the horse trough and washed his hands and face before running to the house. He knew better than to go into Mrs. McKenzie's house looking like a beggar.

Four years earlier, when he had come to Errogie, he did look the worse for wear. Bedraggled and covered in soot and dirt, he certainly looked the part of a beggar. He had done his best to change his appearance in the off chance he came across someone who had known him as McDougal. His long curly red locks had given way to a bald scalp. To replace the hair loss on the top of his head, he had grown a long mustache and goatee. As he approached the McKenzie cottage, Mrs. McKenzie, brandishing her broom, told him to bugger off! His kind were not welcomed there. He explained to her the story he had created to cover his tracks. One evening, while returning home from a late fishing outing, he found the cottage he and his father shared ablaze. He rushed in to try to save his da, but it was too late and he barely made it back out alive. All their possessions were destroyed and he had no living relatives to turn to. So, not wanting to stay in the area where his father died, he wandered south until he came to the village of Errogie where he hoped to start again. McKenzie stepped out of the shadows having heard 'Douglas' story.

"I heard about an old man up north being burnt up in his home. McDougal was the name?"

"Yes sir that was my da."

"All right boy. I could use some help around here. You can sleep in the barn and work for me. You get breakfast and supper and not complain. If you don't do right by me, I'll kick your arse back to the highlands. Or, if I'm really unhappy, I'll let the missus do it for me!"

It took all of McDougal's willpower not to tell McKenzie off. Even though he appeared to be 25 years old, in reality he was 84.

(I'm old enough to be his father and he speaks to me like this!) Thought McDougal. (I'd like to teach him a thing or two!)

(McDougal, you need to calm down! You know he doesn't understand what's happening.)

(Mar-sa-Len, this is hard to do! How am I ever going to get used to this?)

(Patience my friend, it will come to you in time.)

(Luckily, I have plenty of that!) Thought McDougal.

The arraignment worked out well for all. McKenzie got some much-needed help around his homestead, 'Douglas' had the cover story he needed, and Elspeth had a new friend. Plus, by sleeping in the barn away from the family,

Douglas could sneak away at nights to check on the Tacharan. It was a six-mile hike from Errogie to the loch, but Douglas liked the fact that it was far removed from where he was staying. The only one suspicious of Douglas' story was Mrs. McKenzie.

"I tell ya, I don't trust Douglas." She said. "I heard that McDougal lived alone and had no bairns."

"And who told this to ya woman?" Asked McKenzie. "The cackling hens you meet with in the village?"

"They aren't 'cackling hens', but yes. The women in the village heard about the fire, and the stories don't match up!"

McKenzie said, "Well, until I have reason to disbelieve him, I'll listen to the man that was actually there instead of a bunch of nosy gossipers who should be caring for their families instead of making up tall tales! Besides that, he's a good help around the farm."

The missus thought to herself, 'Well if he isn't going to do it, I guess I'll need to keep an eye on Douglas myself.'

A week later, while lying in the barn after a long, hard day of clearing some new land that McKenzie wanted to plant, Douglas heard a familiar voice in his mind.

(McDougal! Can you hear me?)

(Yes Mar-wa-Len! I hear you. Is everything ok?)

(I think so, but there has been a lot of activity on the loch lately. One of the young is close to air breathing, and she surfaced to try. Unfortunately, there were some fishermen in their boats who saw her. Luckily, she swam away before they got too close, but today there are humans swarming the loch!)

(OK, first as you know, keep them in the trenches until this blows over. We've had worse to cover. I'll come up in a day to smooth things over. I still have a stash of coins hidden with you, yes?)

(Yes, and I can always send for more gold if you need it McDougal. Please hurry!)

(I will, and remember, I'm Douglas now. See you soon my friend.)

"What do you mean, 'you've gotten word from home?" I thought you didn't have a home anymore!" said McKenzie.

"I didn't either. But it turns out, an uncle of mine came looking for my father. When he heard what happened, he sent a messenger out to find me. I just got the message last night."

"So?" said Mrs. McKenzie. "And where is this messenger? Where is the letter?"

"He told me the message and left. I can't read, so I didn't see the need to keep the letter."

"Look boy, you know we have a new field to plant. I can't spare you right now. No, it's settled. You'll stay here and maybe in a couple of months, you can go check on this uncle of yours."

"But I can't wait months! He is there now and I must go meet him. Ye cannot keep me here. I've worked hard for you and owe ya nothing." I'll be leaving here within the hour. I've just told you to be honorable."

"Well good riddance to ya boy!" said the Mrs. "I didn't want ya here to begin with!" and with that she stomped outside.

McKenzie bowed his head because he knew Douglas was correct. "I'll miss your help boy, never mind what she said. Plus, I know Elspeth will miss you as well. Go into the kitchen and wrap up some bread and cheese for your journey. Can't have ya show up for lost family starving, can I? When you're done with your uncle, and if ya want to, yer welcomed back here."

"Thank ya Sir, I do appreciate it. Take care and give Elspeth a hug for me please."

True to his word, Douglas was on his way to Loch Ness within the hour. He never did return to Errogie.

(I'm on my way Mar-wa-Len!) Thought Douglas. (Hold fast and I'll be there in a couple of hours. Are the bairns okay?)

(Yes McDougal, I mean Douglas. Since no one can hear me but you, can't I still call you McDougal? I told you I like it better, no offense to your father!)

Douglas chuckled. (Yes, my friend. Call me anything you wish. I'll answer to it for you.)

Mar-wa-Len mentally directed Douglas to the center of activity. As Douglas approached the loch, he heard arguing amongst the locals.

"I'm telling ye, I saw at least three of them beasties swimming about me boat! I swore they were going to smash me to pieces!" said Malcolm.

"Your daft man! I was right here as well! There was only one and it was a wee thing at that. Probably Nessie's bairn." Said Doyle.

"Ach! I think you are all mad! The winds been howling like a banshee all week. The wind mixed with your imagination and whisky is making fools of ya. You saw nothing but waves crashing into one another." Said Angus.

(So.) Thought Douglas. (One is a teller of tall tales, another is truthful, and the third is a skeptic. I need to convince the first two that my skeptical friend is correct. By the sight of them, it's going to take a lot of drink at the closest pub.)

"Hallo friends!" Douglas called. "What's all the commotion about?"

"And who do ye think ye are coming up on us like this?" said Malcolm. "A man can get run through being where he doesn't belong!"

"Easy my hot-headed friend!" said Doyle. "But quickly boy, tell us your name and where yer from."

"I meant no harm, just heard about a monster sighting. My names Douglas. I'm a farmer from Errogie. Have you truly seen the beast?"

"Depends on who yer asking that of." Said Angus. "These two are always seeing fairies and beasties and hearing bumps in the night. Don't take too much mind of them."

"But this time it's true I tell ya!" insisted Doyle.

(Mar-wa-Len! Good news! The two that saw our young one aren't taken seriously it seems.)

(Wonderful McDougal! Now if we can just stay hidden until transport time, we should be in the clear. Three more earth months, and these two will get to see their true home world!)

"I'd love to hear all three of your stories." Said Douglas. "How about a round on me at the closest pub?"

Angus laughed, "I think these two have already had enough, but I don't think any of us will turn you down!"

Three drinks later, Malcolm and Angus were in much better spirits while Doyle was getting angrier about the situation.

"I tell ya, I saw what I saw and no one can tell me different! It was Nessie's babe not waves, not wind!"

Angus replied, "Look my friend we all know you canna swim. There's no harm in admitting you were fearful of tipping over in a storm. Now be honest, did you actually see the beast or did ye just feel your boat arockin?"

"Well" said Doyle sheepishly, "It was dark. I saw the waves cresting over the bow. Can't rightly say it was or wasn't just the water."

"Was there any damage to your boat?" asked McDougal.

"Aye a bit. Lost my nets overboard and sprung a leak. Gonna take me awhile to pay for that."

"Well tell ye what. Maybe it's the alcohol talking, but I've got some gold I can give ye to fix your boat up. Don't want to see ye starving come winter because of some storm damage!" said McDougal.

"I canna take yer gold tho I appreciate the offer. I don't abide charity." Said Doyle.

"What if we consider it a loan?" asked McDougal. "I'll be back this way in a couple of years. Ye can pay me back then."

"Well" said Doyle, "If it's just a loan I can see my way clear to accept yer proposal!"

(Nice work McDougal! You really smoothed this situation over well!)

(Thank you, thought McDougal, it went better than I hoped.)

CHAPTER SIX

Earth Year 1714

Douglas never returned to Errogie (not once planned on it), never recovered his 'loaned' gold (he didn't need it).

Instead he spent the last 78 years wandering around Scotland. Keeping watch over dozens of Tacharan youths, deflecting stories of monsters, and creating false sightings to discredit the real ones.

One of his favorite hoaxes was in 1694. There was a lot of interest in "the Beastie" and so Douglas went to the southeast area of Loch Ness far away from the breeding site. There in the dead of night he constructed a monster. He lashed a few logs together, piled a mound of earth upon it, and fixed a dead doe to the front of his contraption.

Pushing it out into the loch, and seeing it by the full moon, it certainly looked like a creature swimming across the waters. Without horns, the she-deer's profile bore a somewhat effective resemblance to a Tacharan.

Nearby in the village of Alltsigh, the night watch was trading off.

Connor asked Bruce, "Been quiet then yea?"

"Aye it has." Replied Bruce. "But with all the talk of war, I've been jumpy as can be plus if that wasn't enough, I hear that the beast has been spotted again!"

"Oh come on!" snorted Connor, "Tell me you don't believe that foolishness!"

Bruce said, "Do you know for sure that it's not for real? If not, I'd be careful what you say, especially this close to the water!"

Connor said, "Enough of this talk! You need to go sleep off your ignorance and I need to make my rounds." With that Connor turned around and looked out on the water in time to see "The Beast" swimming by.

"Good Lord have mercy!" Yelled Connor as he crossed himself repeatedly. "The Beast is here!"

"Ok" said Bruce. "I get your point. I won't talk about it again."

"Look!" exclaimed Connor pointing out to Ness.

Bruce turned and saw it too. "Oh my Lord in Heaven protect us!" He said in a whisper. "Do we sound the alarm?" he asked Connor.

"I don't want to attract its attentions to us."

Just then the raft made by Douglas lost its momentum and stopped in front of the men. "It's stopping!" said Connor, "It's going to destroy us!"

"I don't think so" said Bruce, "I hadn't heard of the beast destroying whole villages."

"I've heard that and worse." Said Connor. "Run into Alltsigh and quietly gather the men. Tell them to bring weapons. We won't let the monster have our homes without a fight! I'll stay here and keep an eye on that thing."

Bruce ran off while Connor stood there wondering how it would feel to be killed by that giant beast. 'Funny how it's not moving.' He thought. 'Is it thinking about attacking? Did it fall asleep? And it's so quiet!'

Bruce soon returned with the men from the village. They all gasped when they caught sight of Nessie staring across the water at them.

"What do we do?" asked one. "I'm not swimming out there to meet it!" He stated.

"We need to attract its attention to get it to swim over here!" Yelled another.

"I'll do it!" Connor said, and with that he walked down to the water's edge. He picked a branch from a downy birch tree and while slapping the water with the branch, he began to yell at the beast.

"Hey ya great beastie! Come and get me ya lummox!"

But despite Connors yelling and thrashing about, Nessie stayed put. He turned, looked at the others, and shrugged his shoulders. "Now what?" he said.

"Can we throw a rope around her and drag it to shore?" suggested one villager.

"More likely she'll wake up and drag us to a watery grave." Said another.

"Bruce said, "Well we aren't getting anywhere doing nothing. Someone fetch a long rope. Let's try to bring it to shore."

A moment later the requested rope was handed to Bruce. He fashioned a noose and tossed it toward the beast. His hands were shaking so badly that he missed the first three times.

On the fourth toss, he got the rope around its neck. With a cheer the villagers gathered around and grabbed the rough, crudely made rope. They slowly began to pull the beast to shore.

"Why isn't it fighting us?" Asked Connor. Many voices around him muttered their agreement.

As the beast moved closer to shore and into the moonlight, they could tell something wasn't quite right.

One man said, "That's a floating island! Just a mound of earth and some rubbish. What is this trick?"

When the raft struck the shore line the deer head fell to one side.

"We have been made a lot of fools!" exclaimed Bruce. "Someone went to a lot of trouble for us."

Douglas stood in the back of the crowd and grinned. He knew this would settle things down for a while, but now he needed to address the situation as quickly as possible with the young ones.

The crowd of villagers broke up. Some were angry, others relieved, a few were sad that they had not discovered the monster. No matter what they were feeling, Douglas and Mar-wa-Len were pleased with Douglas' deception. (You did very well my friend.) Thought Mar-wa-Len. (Word of this will spread quickly and some will lose interest. This story will be passed down for generations and sew doubt for a very long time!)

(That's wonderful!) Thought Douglas. (Anything to help our cause!)

CHAPTER SEVEN

Earth Year 1715

(War is brewing in Scotland Mar-wa-Len. I think when this bairn is ready to go home we should lay low for a bit.) Thought Douglas.

(Sounds good.) Replied Mar-wa-Len. (What will you do?)

Douglas answered (I've been living around the Loch for over 140 years. It's probably past time for me to disappear for a while as well. I've been thinking about Canada. I hear it's beautiful there and no one knows me. Once things settle down here, we can resume our operations.)

Mar-wa-Len thought (A sound plan Douglas. I'll give you enough gold for your transportation and to get you settled in Canada. Then we can make plans.)

(Thank you.) Replied Douglas. (How long before the youngling is ready?)

(Two more earth weeks and then I'll transport him.)

(Good. That gives me time to arrange my passage and come up with a new identity.)

Douglas decided to shave his mustache and goatee and grow his red curls back. When Mar-wa-Len saw him, she thought (You look just as I first met you! Your hair is shorter, but you're the McDougal I remember!)

(Not McDougal or Douglas anymore. Now I'm Robert Mitchell. That's more of a proper New World name.)

(I like it.) Thought Mar-wa-Len. (Still simple by our standards, but it has a good sound to it.)

(I'm glad you approve.) Laughed Robert. (Of course for you, I'll always answer to anything.)

(Thank you my friend. It's time for me to send the young one home. I haven't decided yet if I'll go with him or stay here. I miss Mothan, but Ness feels like home also. Perhaps I'll go back for a little and come back to Scotland once in a while to check up on events. It will also be easier to communicate with you while I am on earth.)

(Whatever you decide is fine with me as long as you come back when the young need a guardian.)

(I promise I will not give up my duties.)

(Good then. Godspeed my friend. Until we see each other again!)

Robert finished gathering his supplies for the long ocean journey. The trip would take almost two months to sail from Glasgow to Montreal. He had enough funds to sail first class, and as tempting as it was, he decided not to draw any unnecessary attention to himself. He decided to travel mid-ship. Not with the upper class, but definitely not steerage with the lice and filth and disease below decks.

It would cost him to have a private stateroom, but it was well worth the money for the privilege. It also kept him from having to inter act with many other travelers and help keep his story straight. The price included a small amount of food and water, so having the private cabin also gave Robert a place to store his extra provisions without too much worry for theft. Plus the rats weren't as bad on his deck as they were below.

Arriving at the docks, he saw the **HMS Falcon** which would be his home for the ocean voyage. She was a three-mast schooner looking the worse for wear.

"Don't let her fool ya pal." Said a deckhand boarding the ship. "She's the fastest ship sailing to the New World these days. You couldn't be in finer hands!"

"I hope you are right," replied Robert. "She looks like she's about to fall apart!"

The passage was relatively uneventful. The usual amount of fights amongst passengers or between crew members. Storms battered the ship twice, once without incident, the second with some minor ship damage and the loss overboard of two of the crew. Neither of which seemed to bother the captain much. A couple of the young male steerage passengers were conscripted into working their fare off as deckhands.

The arrival at Montreal saw dreadful weather, but spirits were high at seeing land after such a long journey. Robert quickly gathered his possessions and departed the ship.

Robert decided his best plan of attack would be to get away from the larger populated areas and try to find work on a farm since as "Douglas" he had years of experience in that field.

First though, more than anything, he wanted a hot bath, a shot of whisky, a real meal, and a comfortable bed and he didn't care what order they came in. His legs were shaky and his head was swimming from the long ocean voyage and the solid earth of Canada was not only foreign to his knowledge, it also felt foreign to his body.

Following the crowd into town, Robert was feeling overwhelmed. 'I'll be glad to be back on a farm.'

He thought to himself. 'There are too many people here for my liking.'

The population in Montreal was approaching 3000 souls, three times the number he was used to in Inverness and ten times some of the small villages he had lived in. He couldn't look anywhere without seeing people buying, selling, laughing, or rushing around. The streets were lined with food sellers, fur traders, and travelers coming and going. And what a variety of smells! Good food, rotting food, horses and their droppings. Sweat from the workers and perfumes from the 'ladies'. Smoke from cooking, pipe smoke, and fires to keep warm. Two pubs directly across the street from each other were competing to see which could be the loudest. The music, laughter, and shouting seemed to crash into each other at the streets center.

'At least the extra 100 plus years has given me time to learn how to read.' He thought as he studied the signs of the various business establishments lining both sides of the main street. Finally one sign caught his eye.

MRS. CAMPBELLS
BOARDING HOUSE

'Ah!' he smiled to himself. 'Finally a fellow Scot!'

Upon walking through the door, Robert was greeted by the smells, sounds, and sights of a true Scottish Pub.

The inn smelled of pipe tobacco, whisky, beer, and delicious foods cooking. In one corner, a trio of musicians were playing a guitar, a fiddle, and a flute. The melody was one of Roberts's favorite Scottish ballads that brought back many fond memories.

THE PARTING GLASS

Of all the money e'er I had, I spent it in good company.
And all the harm I've ever done,
Alas! it was to none but me.

And all I've done for want of wit,
To mem'ry now I can't recall
So fill to me the parting glass, Good night
and joy be with you all
So fill to me the parting glass,
And drink a health whate'er befall
And gently rise and softly call,
Good night and joy be with you all

Oh, all the comrades e'er I had, They're sorry for
my going away, And all the sweethearts e'er I had,
They'd wish me one more day to stay,
But since it falls unto my lot,
That I should rise and you should not,
I gently rise and softly call,
Good night and joy be with you all.

If I had money enough to spend,
And leisure time to sit awhile,
There is a fair maid in this town,

61

That sorely has my heart beguiled.
Her rosy cheeks and ruby lips,
I own she has my heart in thrall,
Then fill to me the parting glass,
Good night and joy be with you all.

A man may drink and no be drunk.
A man may fight and no be slain
A man may kiss a bonnie lass.
And aye be welcome back again
But since it has so ought to be,
By a time to rise and a time to fall
Come fill to me the parting glass.
Good night and joy be with you all

So fill to me the parting glass,
And drink a health whate'er befall
And gently rise and softly call,
Good night and joy be with you all

But since it fell unto my lot That I should
rise and you should not
I gently rise and softly call
Good night and joy be with you all
Good night and joy be with you all

Around the hall on all the walls were sketches of towns and sights of Scotland. Roberts's eyes were drawn to one image in particular. It was of Urquhart Castle on the shores of Loch Ness. His heart rose for a moment and his throat tightened as he thought of his far away homeland with a painful longing.

"Ach ye fool!" he said aloud. "Get over yer self!"

"And who do ye think yer talking to like that?" He heard behind him.

He turned around to see a stout woman about sixty years old. She was as round as she was tall, fiery red hair streaked with dirty white strands. Her apron was stained with the day's menu of food and drink.

"Begging yer pardon Mrs." He said. "I was admonishing only myself. Feeling a wee bit homesick for Scotland."

"Never apologize for missing that part of heaven boy. Nowhere on earth can take her place. I'm Mrs. Campbell. This is my boarding house. Sit down and I'll bring ye some food and drink, and after that, you'll have a hot bath and get some rest."

"Yes ma'am. Thank you!" Said Robert.

As she bustled away, Robert sat down and watched the crowd. Mostly men looking the worse for wear. Obviously they were just coming in from working various jobs around the area. There were a few women, none of them "professionals", Mrs. Campbell would never allow such behavior in her home. They were the clothes washers and seamstresses, the farm women and street side food sellers. There were also two orphans that Mrs. Campbell had taken off the streets before they froze to death last winter. They were playing a game of jackstones near the fire.

The warmth, and smells, and familiarity were lulling Robert to sleep when Mrs. Campbell came back with a heaping plate of haggis, neeps and tatties. She also was balancing a large mug of ale and a shot of whisky.

"Wake up and eat up boy!" She said. "And betwixt bites tell me aboot yerself."

Robert sat up and smiled with glee at the feast before him.

"Thank you Mrs., Campbell! I haven't had anything even close to this in months!"

"Well dig in boy." She beamed. "Tell me first, what's yer name?"

"I'm Robert, Robert Mitchell." He said between mouthfuls. "I was born in Inverness but I moved around a lot. Mostly worked farms, hoping to do that here."

"That's honorable work Robert." Mrs. Campbell said. "You'll find a lot of farms just outside of town. Don't rightly know if any are looking for help at the moment seeing as how it's not planting or harvesting season."

Robert looked around the inn. "Are you the only one who works here?" he asked.

She replied, "Aye. My son Thomas used to be here to help me a bit. I also had a girl who helped with the cleaning and serving. Elizabeth was her name. She was born in the American colonies, but her family was from the islands in the Caribbean. Sweet girl, very helpful. My son Tom took quite a liking to her and they went and got married. Still they stayed on here and helped. That is until Tom got a wild hair up his arse and took off for the colonies. Some place called Philadelphia or some such. He heard about an inventor named Franklin and wanted to try to apprentice with him. I think he is daft, but he's so hard-headed just like his Da was."

"Where's your husband now, if I can ask?" said Robert.

"He passed on the first winter we got here." She replied. "Died from consumption the doctor said. I don't believe it tho. I just think he couldn't live away from Scotland. Once we got here, he just started wasting away."

"Maybe he caught it during the voyage over here?" Robert reasoned.

"Maybe" she agreed. "But I think it was sadness just as much as anything. Anyway, enough of this! Finish up yer food and I'll go draw yer bath."

Robert tore into the food and ate until he thought his stomach would burst. The atmosphere, drink, and full stomach were making him sleepy again when Mrs. Campbell returned to take him upstairs.

"The bath is drawn, there are some of Tom's old clothes on the bed for ya. Bathe and get some rest. We'll talk more in the morrow. G'night now."

"Thank ye agin Mrs. Campbell. I need to pay you for today tho." Robert replied.

"We'll settle up in the morn. I expect you might stay a bit until you get yer bearings, so we can work out what you owe me later."

"Sounds good to me." Yawned Robert. "Have a pleasant night ma'am."

Mrs. Campbell left and Robert quickly undressed and got into the tub. The hot water scaled his long overdue and unwashed skin. The homemade lye soap rubbed his body a bit raw, but it felt good to be clean once again. Once he was bathed, dried off, and dressed Robert climbed into the softest bed he had ever known. His thoughts turned to the Tacharan. 'Be safe my friends. I miss you Mar-wa-Len.' He thought as he drifted off to sleep.

The next morning, when Robert opened his eyes, he had to pause to remember where he was. As he recalled the night before, he smiled to himself. 'I haven't felt at home like this in quite a while.' He thought. 'Mrs. Campbell could be my own ma if I weren't three times her age.' His stomach rumbled at the smells coming from the kitchen downstairs. He couldn't quite place all the delicious odors, but he knew whatever it was, if Mrs. Campbell made it, it must be good.

As he came down to the dining hall, he saw mostly other boarders eating and getting ready to go off to their jobs. Everyone seemed in good spirits and were enjoying their meal.

"Ah Robert!" beamed Mrs. Campbell. "I trust you slept well? That's probably one of the most comfortable beds in the whole town. Tom had that bed special made for himself seeing as how he was such a big strapping fellow. I think he almost cried when he realized he couldn't take it with him." She laughed.

"Well I for one am glad he couldn't!" said Robert. "I slept like a babe."

"Are ye ready for yer first Canadian breakfast?" she asked. "I have sweet corn pancakes, Canadian bacon, fried cod, oats, coffee, and beer. And of course, maple syrup."

"Ok," Robert stammered. "I'm not sure which I want yet." Trying to decide.

"Just sit down boy!" Mrs. Campbell ordered. "Yer gonna get and eat all of the above."

Breakfast was of course just as good as it smelled. Robert couldn't remember a time that he in any of his many incarnations had eaten so well.

"Now," said Mrs. Campbell. "Let's talk aboot yer plans. I've made some inquires for ya while ya slept. There's not a farm within a hundred miles looking for help right now. So, unless you've got some hidden talent ya haven't talked aboot yet, yer gonna have to come up with another way to earn yer keep."

"Well, I do have enough money for the meantime." Said Robert. "My family and friends all chipped in to make sure my move here went right. Maybe one of the shop keepers in town could use a hand?" he asked.

"I do know of a place needing a hand." She answered. "The work can be tough and the coin isn't a lot, but you'll be treated better there than most places."

"That's great!" Robert replied. "Where would that be?" he asked.

"Right here!" she responded. "Since Tom and Elizabeth ran off on me, I've been busting my arse keeping up with this place. I could use a good strong young man around here. You'll get room and board and a little coin to spend or save, whichever you please."

"That certainly is a tempting offer and I am much obliged to you for it. I just hadn't thought about staying in such a crowded area." He replied.

"Tell me honest Robert, why did you come to Canada? Are ye here to make a clean start, did ye come here to hide from someone or something back home? Yer not a criminal are ye? No, I don't think that's it. Speak up boy, what is it?"

"It's nothing bad I assure you." Robert wanted to be as honest as he could with such a kind person, but he knew she wouldn't understand the complete truth. "The fact of the matter is, my family is all gone. Either dead from disease or in battle. The last straw was my father dying when our house burnt down. I just needed to get away from all the tragedy and this sounded like a good way to start

71

fresh. I'm just not sure about getting too close to anyone quite yet. I hope you can understand."

"Oh, I understand just fine son." She sympathized. "As you know, I've lost my husband, my only son has gone off, and all my other kin is back in Scotland. I've been on my own and alone for quite some time."

Robert looked long and hard around the room. "Maybe" he said slowly, "Just maybe we should stick together for a while. That is until you get tired of me being around." He grinned.

Mrs. Campbell laughed. "It's settled then! Finish yer meal and I'll show you around. You'll work hard I promise, but you will be at home here."

In his heart, Robert knew she was correct. However, he did worry about the future and wondered how hard it would be to move on when the time came. 'You've done it plenty of times before.' He thought. 'It should be easier each time, but somehow it isn't. Oh well, I'll cross that bridge when I come to it. For the time being, this is going to be right.'

It took Robert a few months of working at Mrs. Campbell's boarding house to get comfortable that no one knew his true identity. For quite some time, he felt eyes on him like he was being studied. He eventually understood that every newcomer to this town was subjected to the same scrutiny and that there was nothing special about him to these people. Then one afternoon, it happened.

"McDougal?! Hey McDougal! Is that you?!" Yelled a mountain of a man standing in the front doorway.

Robert slowly turned around. His blood running ice cold through his veins. 'Who on this earth would know him as McDougal?' he thought. 'McDougal has been "dead" for years!'

As Robert finally turned enough to see the speaker, another man sitting behind Robert stood up and rushed to meet the new arrival at the door.

"Cousin!!" he said. "Ach it's good to finally see you! Did ye just get off the ship from Scotland?"

Robert didn't comprehend anymore of their conversation. His blood melted back into his system and was pounding out a rhythm in his ears so loud that it was all he could hear. His heart felt as if it was ripping out of his chest it was beating so hard and fierce. His legs about gave way as he sat hard in a chair.

Mrs. Campbell saw him about to collapse and she ran to his side.

"Robert!" she yelled at him. "Robert! Can ye hear me boy? What is it? You look as if you've see yer own ghostie! Robert! Speak to me son!"

Robert looked at her with glazed eyes. "Can ye please bring me a whisky?" he asked. "Maybe two?"

"Aye. I'll be right back. Sit tight." She replied.

She returned swiftly with a bottle and two glasses, filled them both and sat next to him. Pushing a glass towards Robert she said, "Drink that and tell me what's wrong."

Robert quickly downed the burning liquid, coughed and drew a heavy sigh, knowing once again he had to lie to this kind woman.

"The man that just came in. He looks exactly like my dead father. I thought I was seeing an apparition. And then the name he called, McDougal. That was my father's brother's name. He was killed at the Battle of Dunkeld in 1689. I was only nine at the time, but he was my favorite uncle."

"I am sorry boy. That must have been a shock to be sure." She quietly said. "But ye gotta know, McDougal is quite a common name around Scots. Yer sure to be hearing it agin."

"I know. I just wasn't ready for it I guess. I'll be fine now. I'm sorry for the fright I gave you."

"We'll not speak of it agin Robert, all is well. Why don't you go upstairs and wash up a bit, hmm?" I've got things under control down here. Run along now."

"Yes ma'am, thank you." He replied and headed up to his room.

He laid down on his bed and closed his eyes and thought, (Mar-wa-Len. How I need to talk to you! I wish you could hear my thoughts right now!) But there was no reply.

'She's probably back on her home planet.' He thought to himself. Now feeling sorry for his situation, he pondered the future. 'I'm immortal, but I have no reason to be. I don't have the Tacharan to help, I can't tell anyone about what's happened to me. They'll either think I'm looney and lock me up or think I'm a witch and try to kill me! What am I ever to do?'

Exhausted from the days stress and worry, Robert fell into a troubled sleep. He dreamed of the Tacharan being killed on their home planet while he watched helpless to assist them. He saw the Raiders sweeping over Scotland in their battle cruisers laying waste to every town and village he had called home in the last 150 years. Everyone he had met was burned to a cinder before his very eyes. Young William, the one who set him on this adventure to begin with. Jal-sa-Lem, his first Tacharan friend. Elspeth and her father and mother the McKenzie's burning in their farmhouse. Then the threesome at the loch, Doyle, Angus, and Malcolm. He watched as they sat in the pub, laughing, drinking, and roasting alive.

He could hear them calling to him, asking for his help.

'McDougal, Help!'

'Douglas, Help!'

"Robert! Robert! Robert, wake up boy! Wake up!"

He opened his eyes to see Mrs. Campbell standing over him with a frightened look upon her face. She said, "You were screaming something dreadful son. Everyone downstairs could hear ya. Something aboot being on fire. Were ye having a nightmare aboot yer father's death?"

He shuddered as he remembered the images that had passed through his mind. "Yes, yes I was. It must have been brought on by seeing that man downstairs. I've caused you too much grief today Mrs. Campbell. I can't begin to tell you how badly I feel for bringing this upon you. You've been nothing but wonderful to me."

"Hush boy. We all have our demons to contend with. It never completely goes away, but it will get better. In time you'll learn how to cope with it, just as we all do."

"I'd like to take a week away from town if you don't mind ma'am. I swear I'll come back. I just feel the need to be alone for a few days to clear my head."

Mrs. Campbell lowered her gaze, so Robert couldn't see her eyes water. "Are ye sure yer not running away a'gin? She asked.

"No, truly. I need to sort things out and put the past behind me."

"All right boy. She replied. I'll fix you up some vittles for yer time away. Pack a bag and bedding. But I'm telling ye right now. If I don't see you back here in one week, I'm coming after ya! I know I've fed you more than you've worked for, so ya owe me!" She said with false anger and a wagging finger.

"Yes, ma'am you have and I will be back to work it off, I swear on my honor as a son of Scotland."

"Alright then. That's good enough for me. I'll see ya off in the morning. Good night for now."

"Good night Mrs. Campbell. And thank you again."

CHAPTER EIGHT

Earth Year 1715

Somewhere in the wilderness between

the Canadian and British Colonies

Robert had been wandering for three days, enjoying the peace he felt in the woods. He had stopped at a couple of small settlements but preferred the solitude to company right now.

He contemplated his future. 'What am I to do now?' He thought. 'I don't know when the fighting will end back home, if it ever will. The Tacharan are gone and I have no way to contact them. Am I just destined to live forever wandering the earth?'

(Hello Robert!) He heard. (I've been searching for you!) Jal-sa-Lem thought to him.

"Jal-sa-Lem!" Robert yelled aloud. "Where are you?"

(Behind you friend.)

Robert spun around like an out of control top, almost losing his balance.

"I canna believe my own eyes! Is it really you?" Robert asked incredulously.

(Yes my friend, it is I. But you are so loud!) Jal-sa-Lem joked.

(My apologies, it's been a while since I've 'thought' to anyone and so long since I've seen you! How have you been, and how is Mar-wa-Len?) Replied Robert.

(No worries. I'm happy to see you as well. I'm well. Mar-wa-Len is doing fine and part of the reason I've come over here. How have you been?) Asked Jal-sa-Lem.

(It's been alright, but I've missed you and helping your people.) Answered Robert. (How did you find me? When do ye think we can get back to it?)

(As to your first question, I knew you traveled to Canada and because of your transformation I can detect your unique chemistry makeup. You appear different on my scanners from the other earthlings. I flew here and scanned the Montreal settlement and located you. I was contemplating the best way to contact you when you left town. I've been following you since waiting for an opportune moment when I thought it would be the most likely that we wouldn't be discovered. As to your second question, we don't really know how long the hostilities will last.) Thought Jal-sa-Lem. (But regardless, my people do not think it will end well for Scotland. If that is the case, it might not be the wisest course of action for you to return there any time soon.)

(But what about our work? We need to keep going for the good of the Tacharan!) Argued Robert.

(And we will my friend, we will. All successes have set backs, and all successful peoples know when to stand firm and when to bend. We are 'bending' our plans for now. You and I and our leaders will come up with ideas for continuing. For now, we wait and watch events unfold.) Reasoned Jal-sa-Lem.

(Patience is not one of the virtues I was bestowed with.) Thought Robert ruefully. (I will work on it tho. In the meantime, what did you mean when you said that Mar-wa-Len is part of the reason for your visit here?)

Jal-sa-Lem replied, (She has decided that before she returns to Mothan, she wishes to explore more of your world. There is a lake close to here called Champlain that she wants to stay in for a while and I've come to initiate a transportation tunnel there for her.)

(That's great!) Thought Robert. (I'll have her to talk with and make my stay over here that much more enjoyable!) Robert was giddy with joy.

(Yes, the distance from Champlain to Montreal is approximately 160 kilometers, much shorter than other distances you've handled for us. Once you two are in communication, that distance should not hinder your contacting each other. She will also be able to use the tunnel to return to Loch Ness whenever she chooses to keep watch on the situation there.)

(I canna tell you how much today means to me!) Beamed Robert. (I feel new again.)

(I am pleased.) Thought Jal-sa-Lem. (You left Scotland before I had a chance to arrange for our continued communication, so I am grateful that I was able to locate you as easily as I did.)

(I as well. I didn't even consider that. I've had ye and Mar-wa-Len in me head so long, I guess I took it for granted that it would always be so.)

(We can communicate over long distances, but even our abilities have their limitations. But enough of that. I've work to do. In one weeks' time, make your way to the southernmost tip of Lake Champlain. Mar-wa-Len should be there by then and you two can make that important reconnection.)

(I will and thanks again. It was great seeing you my old friend. Mar Sin Leat!) Waved Robert.

So Jal-sa-Lem took off to complete his work on the tunnel for Mar-wa-Len. Robert pondered what he should do.

'Do I head back to Mrs. Campbell early and then take off again to meet up with Mar-wa-Len, or, should I just head to the lake and be late getting back? Either way I don't think she is going to be happy with me. It's probably best just to be late and try to excuse myself with a story. Hopefully she'll just be happy to see me back at all.'

Robert started the hike, not rushing because he knew he had plenty of time. 'It should take me about four days moving slowly to get to the lake.' He thought. 'No sense running there. I'll still be early to meet Mar-wa-Len, but maybe I can talk again with Jal-sa-Lem!' He thought happily.

The journey went without incident and he arrived at Lake Champlain right on his schedule. It was a beautiful sight to behold. The lake was immense! Besides the ocean he had traveled, Robert had never seen a body of water so large. 'It must be 20 times the size of Loch Ness!' He thought not knowing how close he was to the truth.

(Jal-sa-Lem! I've arrived! Are you here?) Called Robert.

(I am friend, you are early. Is all okay?)

(Oh yes.) Replied Robert. (I'm just anxious to see Mar-wa-Len again. You know, my lack of patience and all!) Joked Robert.

Jal-sa-Lem chuckled. (Yes I do know. I can't say I don't mind the company. How was your trip to get here?)

(Uneventful which suited me fine. This lake is enormous! Why don't we switch the breeding of the young over here? We could have multiple guardians watching even more bairns.)

(A worthy thought, but this isn't as perfect of a location as Ness. Yes, this lake is much larger, but we have a few issues. The temperature here is viable less than half the year. The food source isn't as plentiful as Ness and bringing a larger contingent also increases the likelihood of being found out.) Once we can, we will resume our project in Loch Ness.)

(Well I've always said, there's no beating Scotland for anything!) Exclaimed Robert with a grin.

The tunnel was completed on schedule, and with a small rumble, cycled through its initial transport. Soon after, in the dark dead quiet of the colony know as New York, Mar-wa-Len and Jal-sa-Lem broke the cool calm surface of Lake Champlain. As they came ashore, Robert ran to greet them.

(It is so good to see you Mar-wa-Len! Welcome to the New World!) He said.

(McDougal! I have missed you my friend!) She thought back to him.

(How long do ye plan on being here?) Robert asked.

She replied, (Possibly a couple of months. After that, I'll probably want to return to Mothan for a while. I'll stay here long enough to learn of the customs over here. Who knows? Maybe I'll start the monster rumors over here!) She joked.

(Actually) Thought Robert, (That might not be a bad idea! A few well timed sightings and hoaxes over here, plus your absence in Loch Ness, might just do the trick! I can spread the hoax stories from Scotland over here and add to the legend.)

(That's great!) Thought Jal-sa-Lem. (This will create doubt and confusion on both continents!)

(I had better head back to Montreal.) Thought Robert. (Mrs. Campbell is probably thinking that I'm not coming back to her by now. I'll start spreading stories among our customers when I get back. And who knows? Maybe when you go to Mothan, I can go with you? I'd like to meet with your scientists who are working on fixing yer planet.)

(I think that is a splendid idea!) Said Jal-sa-Lem. (Though, you should know that time passes differently in our solar system. There are magnetic fluxes that distort time, so that one of your years on Mothan could be ten years here on earth. You will need to prepare your mind for that.)

Robert replied, (I don't know if I can understand how that happens or what it means, but, I'm open to give it a go!)

Mar-wa-Len thought, (We can discuss it again when the time comes. For now you should really get back to Canada.)

"Well its aboot bloody time ye came back!" Shouted Mrs. Campbell as Robert walked through the front door of Mrs. Campbell's Boarding House in Montreal.

"Yes ma'am," Started Robert. "I am very sorry…."

"Save yer apologies boy, I dunna wan to hear it! Mrs. Campbell said angrily.

"But Mrs. Campbell, truly it wasn't me fault! Robert tried.

"Oh really? Then who's ta blame fer ye leaving me all alone to tend to this place? Tell me quick boy so I know whose ears to box!"

"No Ma'am, it's not like that. I was headed back here with plenty of time to make it, but I got lost in the woods in the colony called New York. I kept wandering around in circles until I came upon a small settlement near Lake Champlain."

"Lake Champlain? Never heard of it." Said Mrs. Campbell her temperature going down a few degrees.

"Yes, well I got my bearings and was getting ready to head here when I heard some men talking about the monster living in the lake!" Said Robert.

At that, some of the men nearby perked up their ears and turned to pay attention.

One man said, "Monster? What kind of monster in the lake? You mean like what's living in Loch Ness?" He chuckled.

Someone joked, "Maybe the beastie left Scotland to get away from the fighting like some of us did!" Scattered laughter sounded around the room.

"That isn't funny at all!" Stated Mrs. Campbell. "Good men have died and are dying for our homeland so I'm tellin ya now to cut it out!"

"Well." Said Robert. "Loch Ness isn't real, everyone knows that. This Lake Champlain tho, it looks real!"

"Oh really?" asked a patron. "I'll have ye know my grandfather saw the beastie with his own two eyes, and if yer tellin' me that he is a liar, well we are gunna have a problem boy!"

"Easy friend!" said Robert. "I'm not saying he was making up a story, but I ken that there are a lot of tall tales and mischievous young-ins tricking good honest folk."

"Seriously? You know of hoaxes? Can ye tell us aboot some!" asked a fur trader sitting nearby.

"Okay, well when I was a wee lad, my da said that there was a monster sighting in a town called Alltsigh. I've never been there me-self, but the night watch rallied the townsfolk to fight off what they thought was the Ness monster coming to destroy their village. Turned out that some idiot had lashed a dead deer to a raft and floated it out to look like a monster! Gave them all a scare at first, but once they saw what it was, not a one of them was very happy!" Robert relayed.

"Ah yes!" Said Mrs. Campbell. I seem to recall a young man from Alltsigh moving over here and telling aboot that. He of course said that he knew it was fake the whole time."

The fur trader said, "Ack! He was probably the first one to shat his trousers!"

The room erupted in laughter.

"Come on then Robert! Tell us another one!"

"Yes!" someone else yelled.

"Let's hear it boy!" came a call from the corner of the bar.

"My seanair told us a story aboot a hoax that fooled a lot of folks for a while. It was probable a hundred years ago by now. Someone alone or with help, caught aboot a dozen eels and lashed them all together in one big line. Then they let them loose in the loch. It was swimming and thrashing aboot. Everyone thought it was the monster till it finally died of blood loss and floated to shore."

"Do ye have more?" asked the fur trader.

"Aye I do." Replied Robert.

"Before ye say anything else, maybe you and I can talk in private." Said a well-dressed stranger.

"And who might you be?" Demanded Mrs. Campbell.

"Oh yes, hello! My name is Sabastian Benjamin and I'm from The New England Courant, a newspaper in the colonies. I've been looking for some interest stories for our readers. This whole 'Loch Ness / Lake Champlain Monster" story sounds great!"

Mrs. Campbell interjected, "Now hold on! Roberts's stories are his own! You'll not be getting anything for free."

"Of course I'll pay you. How's one dollar per story sound? Two dollars if my publisher uses it." Said Sabastian.

Robert stammered, "That sounds amazing! When can we start?"

"You'll start after yer chores are done and not a minute sooner boy." Answered Mrs. Campbell.

"How about we meet here at 8pm?" Suggested Mr. Benjamin.

Robert agreed, "That sounds good to me. Is that okay with you Mrs. Campbell?"

"I suppose so as long as everything is done around here by then."

"Good! I'll see you then." Said Sabastian.

Later than night, in the privacy of his room, Robert started writing down all of the hoaxes he had committed while living around Loch Ness.

'Let's see.' He thought. 'I've already told him about the deer and raft, and then the eels. Then there was the foot prints a few times.' He laughed to himself. 'It was so funny when they found the fake foot I made hidden behind Urquhart Castle! I might have to make up some stories to keep that reporter interested.'

The more he thought about this new development, the more he saw it as a way to protect the Tacharan.

'What if I could get newspaper people in different countries to spread false information?' They could also watch out for true information and let me know about it.' He knew he would need to be selective with the people he chose and trusted. 'There can't be too many people involved, don't want to spread the circle too thin. I'll certainly need to involve the Tacharan in the selection process.'

Thus was the Protectors created. Newspapers were still a novel idea, but growing in popularity around the globe.

CHAPTER NINE

Earth Year 1500

Location: The Tacharan Home Planet
(One hour before the bombs fell.........)

Mak-na-Tal and Cre-na-Tal walked hand in hand across the dense, green landscape surrounding the education complex of Allmhara, the capital city of the Tacharan home world Mothan. The air smelled crisp and clean as usual for their city. Pollution had been eradicated decades ago and the air scrubbed. The sky was a deep purple signaling an early fall season and a mild winter. Life was good and enjoyable for the Tacharan. Days were spent learning and creating, while evenings were dedicated to community and family time activities. The Civil Defense Patrols could be seen wandering around the city. 'I don't understand why we have the CDP anyway." Thought Mak-na-Tal. 'No one here would think of doing the illogical thing of hurting another.'

As they walked, he turned his thoughts to the joy of the last week. Their Joining Ceremony had just taken place less than a week ago, but their duties as Educators at the Halls of Learning kept them from the traditional time of bonding away from the city.

"The Learning Period is ending soon." Said Mak-na-Tal. "Then we will go away for our bonding cycle."

"I look forward to our time." Said Cre-na-Tal.

{ Aboard the Raider Battle Cruiser Tolowar under the Battle Cruiser Lagartheria squadron }

"Captain, our next target is coming into viewer range." Stated First Officer KemChar.

"On screen." Said Captain CadaRon.

"Yes Captain." Answered the helmsman. "On screen."

Everyone on the bridge looked towards the viewer as Mothan appeared before them.

"It's is so green, and blue!" said the helmsman. "This planet will produce much for our people!"

"Control yourself fool!" commanded KemChar. "We all know our mission and what it means. No need for you to open your mouth!"

"Yes Sir, sorry Sir." Said the chastised junior officer.

Captain CadaRon said, "KemChar. Give me a rundown of the resources we should be able to extract from this planet."

"Aye Sir. Readouts indicate 1,386 million cubic kilometers of freshwater. Atmospheric content includes; 78.09% nitrogen, 20.95% oxygen, 0.93% argon, 0.04% carbon dioxide, and small amounts of other gases. Quite similar to our needs. Once we reduce the nitrogen and oxygen to proper levels, we will have an abundance of breathable air for our use."

"Yes of course air and water are desirable" said CadaRon. "But this mission is costing our people a fortune. I want to know that SlayThans plan is going to pay off. Tell me about minerals, valuables, what of them?"

KemChar replied, "There is very little in the way of 'valuables' in their soil content. It will support plant life, but it is worth little else. Our people need the air and water most of all."

"When we are done, this planet won't support plant life at all." noted the captain. "All this way and no platinum? No gold or diamonds? We need those for the trading that we do! SlayThan is a fool." The captain shook his head.

Captain CadaRon said, "KemChar. Raise the Lagartheria and get me Captain SlayThan."

"On viewer Sir!" said KemChar.

"CadaRon! What is it?" asked SlayThan. "I am busy in case you weren't aware."

"Of course, sir" replied Captain CadaRon. "I'm just checking in for the attack. My ship is ready when you give the command."

SlayThan roared, "You mean MY ships are ready! Just because some imbecile gave you a command doesn't mean you are in charge of anything you old fool! This is my mission, my ships, and my glory! You will follow my lead and attack where and when I say!"

"Yes sir" CadaRon gritted his teeth. "On your command!" CadaRon motioned to KemChar to cut the signal and KemChar complied.

"Sir, we are receiving attack coordinates from the Lagartheria." Stated KemChar.

"On viewer." Replied Captain CadaRon.

The captain studied the attack plan devised by SlayThan. "Tell me KemChar. Do you see the flaw I see in this attack?"

"It isn't my place to criticize a ships captains plan Sir." Deflected KemChar.

"Stop the politics and tell me what you see. SlayThan isn't here to kill you, and I certainly won't hold it against you for criticizing him."

"Well" KemChar hesitated, "While his plan does take out the main cities, he is virtually leaving the mountain ranges untouched."

"Correct. And what does that foretell?" asked CadaRon.

"He has either overlooked them, or he doesn't believe the Tacharan would be there. If there are any hidden refuges or tunnel system in place, the Tacharan could easily evade our bombing runs and our ground forces during the mop up." Explained KemChar.

"Good" CadaRon complimented. "I'll make a captain out of you yet. Tell us what you would do differently."

KemChar, warming up to the task said, "I would start the bombing runs in the mountain ranges and bomb inward towards the cities. Thus, herding the Tacharan into the buildings. Next, I would destroy the cities wiping out the vermin. Our ground troops would clean up any stragglers. Then we could take the resources at our leisure without any true resistance or possible retaliation."

"Very good KemChar!" CadaRon exclaimed. "You deserve a captain's chair more than that buffoon SlayThan. Do you want to contact him and point out his errors?"

Eyes wide, KemChar stuttered, "No Sir! I would like to live long enough to get that captain's chair. I'm not quite ready to commit suicide."

CadaRon laughed, "So what do we do? Follow our orders without question, or point out the error and hope for a good outcome?"

KemChar said, "I will defer that decision to you my captain. Me, I'll keep my opinions to myself unless they are asked for. Now that I've expressed my thoughts, it is up to my captain to decide what to do with that opinion."

CadaRon laughed even harder, "KemChar! Are you going for a captain's chair or a seat on the council? That is the most politically correct answer I've heard in a long time!"

KemChar laughed as well, "I'm happy where I am now sir. When another opportunity arises, I'll consider the possibilities. May I asked Sir, are you going to discuss this with Captain SlayThan?"

"No, you may not ask." Replied CadaRon. "I will be in my quarters. Alert me if anything changes to our schedule."

"Yes Sir," said KemChar.

Captain CadaRon sat back at his desk and sighed, contemplating the upcoming battle. 'Not really a battle' he thought. 'These Tacharan don't have any planetary defenses. We will attack and then take what we want just as we always do. This is what we do, it's who we are now. We need to survive as a species, we have that right! Don't we?' he thought.

He knew that SlayThan's plan would not be completely successful but would accomplish the mission of securing the planetary resources.

'SlayThan will look like a hero for the short term.'
He mused. 'But some of them will survive just as
KemChar predicts. When that is found out,
SlayThan will pay for his arrogance. Well good!
He is an obnoxious bastard and he deserves to be
taken down a few pegs.'

'Besides' he thought, 'I don't have anything
against the Tacharan, we used to be friends, we
traded peacefully with them. That is, back when
we had a planet of our own we could live on. Now
we do this to survive, we cannot let our people
fade into history because of our mistake, can we?
If the Tacharan wanted to protect themselves, they
should have weapons, right? So actually, this is on
them just as much as us.' He tried to reason with
himself. 'Now I'm trying to justify destruction
and killing.' He looked at himself in the mirror
over his work station. The once pure red hair was
liberally streaked with grey and the wrinkles
around his eyes were getting deeper. 'SlayThan
may be correct. Quite possibly I am too old for
this anymore. Perhaps this will be my last battle.

KemChar will make a good captain in my absence.'

The attack proceeded as planned by Captain SlayThan. The cities were wiped clean from the planet's surface and the planet was scoured for its resources. SlayThan was quite proud of himself as his squadron returned victorious to the fleet.

Cre-na-Tal huddled in the tunnels with the other survivors, Mak-na-Tal's head cradled in her arms.

"Don't worry my love" she stammered, "You will be alright. Our healers are coming to care for you."

"No dear." Said Mak-na-Tal. "I don't think so. My wounds are much too grievous. Promise me you will do everything you can to ensure the Tacharan survival."

"I swear it to you. I will dedicate my life to the future of our people." Promised Cre-na-Tal. "Now rest my sweet."

With that, Mak-na-Tal closed his eyes, never to open them again. Cre-na-Tal vowed that one day, her people and her world would be whole again.

CHAPTER TEN

Earth Year 1720

New York Colony on the

shore of Lake Champlain

(Mar-wa-Len are ye near?) Called Robert in his thoughts.

(I am here.) Thought Mar-wa-Len. (How are you Robert?)

(I'm well thanks. Things are going splendid. I have a friend in Europe watching the press for us and Sabastian, our newspaper friend here, as well. They are both glad to help as Protectors and deflect any stories.)

(That is good news Robert! I went to Scotland last week and listened to some of the local's thoughts. It is humorous how I'm still being spotted even though I'm not there!)

(Ha! That is funny!) Thought Robert.

(So what has brought you my way?) Asked Mar-wa-Len.

(I was thinking it may be time to take up that offer of a trip to Mothan!)

Mar-wa-Len replied, (That's great! Why now?)

One Week Earlier

"Robert! Come here boy!" called Mrs. Campbell.

Robert came out of the kitchen to see Mrs. Campbell standing by the front door with a young man and young lady.

"Robert, I'd like you to meet my son Thomas and his wife Elizabeth. They've come back from their Philadelphia foolishness."

"Now ma, that wasn't foolishness! I learned a lot. It was a great experience!"

"And what good will it do us, hmm? Tell me that!"

Robert interjected, "Hello Tom! It's great to finally meet you."

Thomas Campbell stood six feet tall, had jet black shoulder length hair, blue eyes and very fair skin. His wife Elizabeth was a contrast with her long curly light brown hair, brown/gold eyes, dark complexion, and only standing at five feet two inches.

"Likewise Robert! Mother has written me about you. Said you were a great help to her in my absence, so thank you!"

"All right! If you two are done hugging, tell me Thomas what are yer plans?" Asked Mrs. Campbell.

"Well." Said Tom. "Ellie and me were thinking about starting a family so we figured to come back here with you."

"You won't be needing me then." Said Robert. "I've been wanting to take a trip to see some old friends, so this is a blessing in disguise."

Mrs. Campbell replied, "I guess it is Robert, but you'll be sorely missed."

"Thank ye ma'am. I appreciate everything you have done for me. I'm sure I'll be back around to see ya."

"Think nothing of it boy. Ye earned everything you got, and I do hope ye won't be a stranger. I've come ta think of ye as me own son."

"Well," said Robert. "I guess you'll be wanting that comfortable bed back so Ill pack up my belongings and get out of yer way Tom."

"No rush," Tom replied. "But I will appreciate a good night's rest in me own bed."

CHAPTER ELEVEN

Earth Year 1720

New York Colony on the shore

of Lake Champlain

part two

Mar-wa-Len thought (I would enjoy taking you to Mothan! Now remember what Jal-sa-Lem told you about the time displacement between our worlds?)

(I still don't understand how that can be, but, yes. He said one year on Mothan could be ten years here? That is so odd!)

(Just so you are prepared for when you come back to earth. We will try to keep you updated on changes here while you are gone. Whenever you are ready, we can use the tunnel.)

(I don't know about using that tunnel of yours tho. I'm not much of a swimmer. Maybe I could go in Jal-sa-Lems ship?) Robert asked.

(I will contact him. In the meanwhile, I'll tell you more about Mothan. I know our people will be excited to meet you!)

(And I'll be able to see the young ones that were raised in Ness?)

(Of course! I'm sure they will be thrilled to see you as well.) Thought Mar-wa-Len. (Pack enough for a while, the trip uses a lot of resources.)

(In that case, maybe I shouldn't go?) Suggested Robert.

(Absurd!) Exclaimed Mar-wa-Len. (You've done more for our people than we could ever repay. You will be more than welcomed!)

(All right then, let Jal-sa-Lem know I want to go to Mothan! In the meantime, if I'm going to be away for a while, maybe Robert Mitchell should meet his demise?)

(I'm sure you can make suitable arraignments for that.) Thought Mar-wa-Len.

(I'll get to it right away so I'm ready when Jal-sa-Lem arrives.)

Robert went off to plan the world's loss of Robert Mitchell. He was planning on just digging a grave and letting everyone believe it was his, when he came upon a dead body in the woods. On closer examination, it was a fairly recent death. Robert looked up and saw what had occurred. His new found 'friend' had lost his footing and fallen down into a 75-foot ravine. Luckily it was a quick death. He had struck his head on a boulder and split his forehead open. The damage was extensive enough to make him unrecognizable.

Robert decided to change his plan. 'I'm going to take this poor fellow into a town, give him a decent burial, and let everyone there think he's Robert Mitchell. Then I'll send Mrs. Campbell a letter informing her of 'Roberts' death.

So Robert bundled up his unfortunate friend, placed him on his horse, and traveled into Albany the nearest town along the Hudson River.

As he came into town, he heard, "You there! What happened? Who are you?"

Robert turned around to see the town's sheriff Shawn Hale.

"Hello! My names Edward. Me and my friend Robert were camping along the Hudson River. Two nights ago Robert went off to relieve himself. I heard him yell and then a loud crash. I went looking but because it was so dark, I couldn't see a thing. The next morning, I found Robert at the bottom of a ravine with his head smashed in."

"I'm sorry about your friend son. What are your plans?" Asked the sheriff.

"Well, I'd like to bury him and send his mom a message. I have money to care for him."

Sheriff Hale directed "Edward" to the undertaker and then to the general store where messages could be sent from.

"Hello." Said Bill Calaway the towns' undertaker. "What can I do you for?"

"My friend is outside on my horse. He is in need of your services. Can you take care of him for me?"

"Of course son, I'm sorry for your loss."

"Thank you sir. I just need a headstone, box, and a grave. There won't be a ceremony, no one here knows him."

"All right. That will be five dollars for the marker, two for the coffin, and I won't charge you for the digging."

"I appreciate that sir. He was a good guy, just take care of him please."

McDougal gave him the name Robert Mitchell for the engraving along with the made up birthdate of November 24th, 1695 and May 1st, 1720 for his death. Then he bid the undertaker goodbye.

He walked across the dusty town street to the general store. There he met Ms. Fink. She was a tall, good looking German woman who owned and operated the general store.

"Good afternoon sir!" She said. "What are you looking for today? I'm sure I have whatever you need."

"Well, I probably do need some supplies for a trip I'm about to go on, but first I need to send a message and parcel to Montreal." He explained to Ms. Fink his story. "Can you handle that for me?"

"Of course I can dear. I have a boy who will ride up there for you. You can write up your message on this paper here. You can write son?"

"Yes ma'am. I also have a bundle of his belongings for his mom."

"Certainly. Here's a burlap sack. Whatever you want to send can go in this. Otto will take it at first daylight tomorrow. It will cost you three dollars. Is that alright?"

"Yes, I can cover that." He replied.

So he filled the sack with some of his own possessions and included $50 which was quite a lot of money for the time.

He also included a note:

Dear Mrs. Campbell,

You don't know me, but my name is Edward Schmidt. I was traveling through the British colonies with Robert when he had an accident and unfortunately passed away. Before he went, he told me about you and how to get in touch with you. I know he would want you to have his possessions. I'm also sending you his life's savings since he didn't have any relatives, though I know he considered you as his family.

I am sorry for your loss.

God Bless,

Edward

"Here's the three dollars Ms. Fink. Thank you for taking care of this for me. I guess I'll look around for my trip now." Said McDougal.

"Take your time son, plenty to see. I can't extend credit seeing as how you don't live here." She replied.

"That's fine ma'am, I have some money saved up."

He thought to himself, 'what am I going to need on Mothan? I've got some clothing, maybe some more for when these wear out. I'll bet they don't have whisky! I'd better stock up on that! I know they have food; we've been sending that thru the transportation tunnel for years.'

He quickly picked out a few shirts and trousers, and a case of Old Bushmills Distillery whisky. 'It might be Irish,' he thought with a grin, 'but it will do.'

He paid for his purchases and headed out of town towards his next adventure.

A week later, in a small clearing east of Lake Champlain, Robert met up with Jal-sa-Lem.

Jal-sa-Lem thought, (Are you ready Robert?)

(Aye, I think so. Tel me again what is this going to feel like? Will it be the same as sailing on the ocean?)

Jal-sa-Lem chuckled, (No, nothing like that rough journey. For the most part, you won't even realize we are moving. Our ships have mechanisms that take away the feeling of motion. If you look out a window, you'll see the stars going by, but other than that, you would never know.)

Robert shook his head and laughed, (We could have used that on the ***Falcon****!)*

CHAPTER TWELVE

Journey to Mothan

As Jal-sa-Lem and Robert made their way to the Tacharan ship, Robert inquired, (How long will this trip take?)

Jal-sa-Lem thought, (Since we aren't in a hurry, I was thinking of showing you around your area of space. Do you know how many planets circle your own sun?)

Robert replied, (No idea. I know the sun, the moon, and earth, but that's it. Mar-wa-Len has mentioned other planets, but they don't make sense to me.)

(Including Earth, you have nine planets and 181 moons, though after your scientists discover those people will debate for years the number and what constitutes a planet or a moon. It never fails. We have seen this play out with many developing cultures.)

(Why is that?) Asked Robert.

(The simple answer is, people love to argue. It seems to be a part of humanoid DNA.)

Robert chuckled, (I think you are right about that! And on that point you'll get no argument from me!)

Jal-sa-Lem laughed, (Thank you!)

Arriving at the ship, they quickly boarded and got ready for their departure. Jal-sa-Lem showed Robert where to store his belongings and familiarized him with the ship.

(This thing still amazes me!) Robert thought. (How is it so white and bright?)

(You will quickly become adjusted to it.) Assured Jal-sa-Lem. (Now let's get strapped in so we can be on our way.)

Even though the ship was built to transport final stage Tacharan, Robert found the seat he was strapped into quite comfortable. The lights began to dim and a faint humming sound was heard.

Robert felt alarmed as the ship started lifting off of the Earth.

(Oh my! Oh my! Oh my!) He called out in his thoughts. (We are moving!)

(Of course we are moving. It's very difficult to go anywhere without moving.) Jal-sa-Lem replied trying to sooth Roberts worries.

(I know that!) Robert thought sheepishly. (I just didn't know what else to say.)

(I apologize. I shouldn't make light of your response to such a new experience. For me this is like swimming across the loch. For you there is no real comparison.)

Robert responded, (No worries my friend. I'm feeling better now. Tell me, is that the moon ahead of us? It's so large!)

(That is your moon but size is relative. It's actually only one fourth the size of your home planet.)

(Amazing! Can we land there and walk around a bit?)

(Not without very special equipment. You see, the moon doesn't have the same air as Earth. One step outside my ship and you would last about 15 seconds before you used up all the oxygen in your body.)

(Alright then. How about we fly around and move on? I'll look from the comfort of me chair and window!)

Jal-sa-Lem laughed, (Whatever you say!)

He proceeded to fly about the planets, explaining to Robert the details about the various spheres floating in space.

When Robert asked for names, Jal-sa-Lem replied, (Well, of the nine planets you know Earth. Five others can be seen by the naked eye if you know where to look and they were named by the Romans.) He proceeded to point out Jupiter, Mars, Mercury, Saturn, and Venus. (There are three more that your people will not find unless they build devices to see distances.)

(This is all truly remarkable, but I've seen enough to fill my brain for a long time. How about we head to Mothan? I think I need a rest.)

(Then rest my friend. I'll wake you if anything exciting happens.)

Robert nodding off and slept soundly for a few hours of uninvaded rest. He awoke refreshed and full of questions.

(So where are we now? How long before we get to Mothan?)

(We are further away from Scotland than you have ever been my friend. Other than that it would be difficult to give you an answer you would comprehend. For your second question, two more days of travel will find us on Mothan. Everyone is quite excited to see you. We have a reception with our Chief Elder Kem-ka-Jen and with Cre-na-Tal our Lead Scientist. They are both looking forward to meeting you.)

(Well I certainly hope I live up to their expectations. If I knew I'd be meeting them I would have brought a better outfit with me.)

Jal-sa-Lem said, (Do not worry about that my friend. There is no concern about your wardrobe. They are anxious to hear your stories and discuss the future with you.)

Robert replied, (That eases my mind quite a bit, thank you. I am looking forward to learning more about your people and how we can help them further.)

CHAPTER THIRTEEN

Mothan

As they flew over Mothan, Robert felt sadness at the barren wasteland that passed beneath his gaze. He had always been surrounded by life; the woods, farms, and people. What he saw was only despair.

(It's so… empty.) He thought.

(Yes my friend. This was a lush vibrant planet much like Earth before the Raiders. Look below now.)

Robert looked down and saw the ruins of a large city. The sands and wind had added to the damage, but he could tell that the concrete and metal structures had been attacked by strong forces. They lay twisted and crushed and scattered across the landscape.

(I wanted you to see this.) Thought Jal-sa-Lem as he circled the wreckage. (This was our capital city of Allmhara. That large tower was the center of our Halls of Learning. Cre-na-Tal and her new mate were standing right there when the attack took place. She was fortunate to survive, he was not.)

Robert felt a lump forming in his throat. Despite the cool clean air in the ship, he began to sweat. Anger built up inside of him until he was ready to burst.

(This is disgusting! How are these animals allowed to live on?) He wanted to know. (Aren't there others willing to destroy these Raiders?)

(Most beings are happy to keep a "hands off" approach to galactic matters. As long as it doesn't affect them, it's best to turn their backs on it. Then there are those like the Raiders who trade with them. They are much too powerful for the Raiders to conquer, so they let them continue their path of destruction as long as the Raiders keep bringing them valuables to trade.) Replied Jal-sa-Lem. (I showed this to you, not to make you angry, but to let you know how important you are to us and what your work has meant.)

They sat back and rode the rest of the way in silence. Jal-sa-Lem guided the ship into a camouflaged cavern and set it down next to two other craft. He quickly shut down the ships systems as Robert went to his quarters to gather his belongings.

The ships hatched opened up to cheers from the gathered crowd, all eager to get a glimpse of their hero.

Robert felt overwhelmed at the response and wanted to go back into the ship. Jal-sa-Lem took hold of his arm and propelled him forward.

(Don't disappoint them Robert. This is the biggest event they have had in decades.)

Robert straightened his shoulders and marched out of the ship to meet the Tacharan.

CHAPTER FOURTEEN

Sanctuary

Robert was lead through the crowd. He had never felt short in his life, but walking through the mass of Tacharan bodies, all of whom were at least a foot taller than him, made him feel small. Every one of them were reaching out to touch this savior of the Tacharan.

Robert thought to Jal-sa-Lem, (Why are they so quiet? I can hear your thoughts, why not theirs?)

(They are trying to be respectful of your privacy. They are anxious to speak with you, but do not want to overwhelm you with so many thoughts at a time. You are used to me and Mar-wa-Len, but this many voices at a time would be deafening. I can hear everyone in our community right now, but I'm able to sort them out. You will learn in time to do this as well.)

They continued on through the chamber until they came to the entrance to the underground Tacharan home.

(Welcome to Sanctuary Robert.) Said Jal-sa-Lem. (This has been our home since the Raiders attacked us and forced us underground.)

The many years of living underground had given the Tacharan time to build a home for themselves, but it had taken its toll on them as well. The lack of fresh air and sunlight had dulled their skin. The leadership worked very hard to keep everyone occupied in some productive manner in the effort to stave off depression.

(We already had an emergency base here before the attack. Mostly military in nature, many felt it was an unnecessary allocation of resources, but now we know better. Over the years, we have expanded Sanctuary to include housing areas, laboratory and research facilities, gardens and hatcheries. We have an education center for our young once they return to us from Earth. The food you and Mar-wa-Len have been sending us was of great benefit. Our people were growing quite tired of our meager diet.) Jal-sa-Lem explained as they toured around the facility. (The gardens and hatcheries also helped our air supply, but we were required to build air scrubbers to keep our oxygen levels high enough to support everyone. Our most pressing issue was our water supply. We knew there would never be enough for breeding, but luckily, we were able to tap into a deep planet reservoir for our needs.)

(Well I think this is a remarkable accomplishment for your people.) Robert replied. (This underground facility is leaps and bounds ahead of anything we have on Earth. I'm sure there isn't a scientist or inventor who wouldn't give up a body part or two to trade places with me right now!)

(Thank you. I am proud of my people for rising up from what has happened to them. In that same spirit, Cre-na-Tal and her team are working on a plan to recreate our planet. They are hoping to work with you since we will need resources from Earth to remake Mothan.)

(Anything I can do to help my friend.)

(Good! For now, let's rest and refresh ourselves. The reception in your honor isn't for a few hours. I'll show you to your quarters where you'll be staying while on Mothan. Your bags have already been sent ahead for you.)

The rooms set aside for Robert were more than he expected for the situation. He had a bedroom, sitting area, and a room he wasn't quite sure of. There was the oddest of chairs, a counter top with a bowl cut into it, and what only could be described as a closet, but the walls were all made from glass.

(This is really more than I need Jal-sa-Lem! I hope I'm not putting someone out. Just a bedroom and directions to the outhouse would be fine.)

Jal-sa-Lem laughed. (These are actually new rooms that were made for you. The benefit of being underground is that if you want another room, you just dig. As far as an outhouse goes, we don't have those.)

(Um, ok. I guess we never discussed that part of our differences and similarities.) Robert stammered. (What should I do?)

Jal-sa-Lem replied, (That's what that room is for.) as he pointed towards the far room. (I will be happy to explain the devices in there.)

As they entered the room, Jal-sa-Lem started to explain what each item did and how to work them. Robert was fascinated by everything.

(You mean to wash up, I don't have to pump the water? And when I need to, use the outhouse, just use that seat? This is absolutely amazing!)

(Your people will eventually invent these items as well. I'm sure you will see other things here that aren't on Earth as of yet.)

Robert thought, (I could take these back to Earth and make a fortune!)

(We can discuss that later. For now, rest up and I'll be back in a couple of hours.)

After Jal-sa-Lem left, Robert gave his new room a complete test. Quite satisfied with the results, he lay down on his bed and drifted off to sleep.

True to his word, Jal-sa-Lem returned on time to take Robert to the reception in his honor.

(Cre-na-Tal and Kem-ka-Jen will of course wish to converse with you so they will be making contact. There are a few others that you should want to speak with also. I have asked them to be mindful of your inexperience with telepathy. Let me know if you are feeling overwhelmed at any time.)

(Thank you, I appreciate that. I am looking forward to speaking with them as well.)

As they entered the grand chamber, the assembled Tacharan began applauding. Robert could feel a swelling in his mind of, what could only be described as, affection. Robert looked ahead and saw a raised platform with two Tacharan seated upon it.

Robert surmised correctly that the larger Tacharan seated in the middle of the platform was the chief elder. Robert thought to himself that this being could only be described as impressive. He would most likely be eight feet tall when standing. His skin had a blue-grey-green mottled appearance that literally glowed. His eyes were a piercing violet that watched Roberts every move. He wore a simple tunic of some sort of plant material dyed yellow. Around his neck he wore an elaborate charm suspended on a silver chain.

Seated to his side and a level lower was Cre-na-Tal. She was slightly hunched and appeared older than the chief though age was difficult to measure for Robert. If she stood upright she was probably six feet tall same as Robert. Her skin was a dull grey and her eyes were a cloudy blue. As he looked around the room, he noticed a number of other Tacharan whose skin was dulled.

Robert thought to Jal-sa-Lem, (Is Cre-na-Tal okay? She looks sick.)

(I'll explain it to you later.) Thought Jal-sa-Lem. (Suffice it to say that everything is as it should be.)

Robert tried to put it out of his mind as they continued to walk forward.

As they approached the podium, Cre-na-Tal and Kem-ka-Jen stood to greet them.

(Welcome most honored guest!) Robert heard in his mind the powerful voice of Kem-ka-Jen. (We, The Tacharan, are blessed by your presence and thank you for your many years of service to our people!)

(Thank you Chief Elder.) Robert thought back. (I am honored to be here and to get to meet you. I certainly don't want anyone fussing over me though.)

Cre-na-Tal responded, (It has been far too long since we have been able to have visitors. You will find that we all wish to meet you and converse with you.)

(Well I do plan on being here for a while, so we will have the time. I especially want to work with you ma'am to try to figure out a permanent solution to your situation.)

Cre-na-Tal nodded. (I look forward to introducing you to my fellow scientists and sharing ideas with you.)

(Enough time later for that!) Said Kem-ka-Jen. (Now it is time to celebrate our friend and protector McDougal! Everyone! Eat, drink!)

The voices grew in Roberts head. Not painfully, but definitely a feeling of fullness. Before he knew it, a plate of food had been thrust into his hands and a cup of a purple drink. Some of the foods were recognizable since they came from earth. There was some lichen native to Mothan that when tried turned out to be quite delicious. He sniffed and sipped the purple colored drink and found it to be amazingly refreshing.

(Jal-sa-Lem! What is this drink? It is wonderful!)

(Ah! That was made in your honor. It is a special occasion beverage that I have not had in many years. It is called Morcha. It is made by boiling grains and fruits and spices together. I am glad you are enjoying it.)

The celebration progressed well into the night. Robert couldn't remember having such a good time in quite a while.

He thought to Jal-sa-Lem, (This has been quite a gathering.)

(Yes it has and it was good for our people to celebrate again. Thank you for being here for them.)

(My pleasure I assure you.) Replied Robert.

(In the morning, I will come get you for morning meal and we have much to discuss. For now, I am quite ready to get some rest.) Thought Jal-sa-Lem.

(Rest does sound good. I'll see you. Sleep well.)

(And you as well my friend.) Jal-sa-Lem thought as he waved his good-bye.

Only once back to his quarters did Robert get turned around. Making it to his room, he sat down on the bed and kicked off his shoes. He thought he would sit up for a while, but without realizing it, he fell asleep and didn't awaken until Jal-sa-Lem came to get him.

(I trust you slept well?) Asked Jal-sa-Lem.

(I did thank you! What's for breakfast? I'm famished! It must be the space travel or the air here, but I think I could eat a horse!) Thought Robert.

Jal-sa-Lem laughed. (No horses here I'm afraid, but I'm sure we can fill your stomach. Come friend.) And with that Jal-sa-Lem turned down the corridor and let Robert to the communal dining hall.

Upon entering the hall, everyone turned to look at Robert. A small sound built up in his mind as the gathered Tacharan thought blessings to him and threatened to overwhelm his brain.

Robert said aloud to Jal-sa-Lem, "It's so loud! Please ask them to stop!"

Jal-sa-Lem raised his hand to the room and thought the command. At his word, the crowd stopped their adoration of Robert and resumed their meals.

"They aren't unhappy with me for stopping them?" Asked a confused Robert.

(No my friend.) Jal-sa-Lem replied returning to thinking. (They understood my message and wish no harm to you. They all promised me to be more careful in the future.)

(Thank you.) Replied Robert. (Speaking of future, what about mine and our mission?)

(I've given this a great deal of thought and I think the best case scenario keeps you here for a while so that you can learn from all of our scientist. If we are ever to rebuild our planet, we are going to need resources from your world and the minds here working together.)

(Sounds great to me.) Thought Robert. (I've got a lot to learn if I'm going to be helpful with rebuilding your planet. Changing paths for a minute, can you tell me now about Cre-na-Tal? Her skin and eyes are so much duller than yours and she looks so tired.)

141

Jal-sa-Lem sighed. "I will speak aloud to you to explain what is happening. The others don't understand your language and this is a personal matter among my people."

"If you can't tell me, just say so. I don't want you to break any promises."

"No its fine, just sensitive." Said Jal-sa-Lem. "It is related to the bonding. When a couple are bonded it is forever. If something happens to one, it is as if it is happening to the other. When Mak-na-Tal was killed, it affected Cre-na-Tal. Fortunately for her, they had not completed the bonding, so she did not die immediately but it has had a profound effect on her. She is no longer immortal, so her body is dying."

"Is that true of the others I saw last night?" asked Robert.

"Yes" was the reply. "Some died within days of the attack, others have lingered. I don't know who to feel the worse for."

Robert asked, "Isn't there anything to be done? This is horrible!"

"Even our science doesn't have an answer for this. No, it is the way of things for us and accepted."

Robert stated, "Well I know the first area of your sciences I wish to study, your body make up! Maybe I can see something you haven't."

Jal-sa-Lem nodded, "Maybe you can. By the way, 'body make up science' is called 'biology'. You'll learn the names of all the areas of study."

"Excellent!" said Robert. "Let's begin!"

Robert spent the next 25 years on Mothan learning everything they could teach him. The more he learned, the hungrier he was for more. Cre-na-Tal and the other Tacharan scientist were impressed with Roberts's ability to absorb information and his developing critical thinking skills. Mar-wa-Len continued her visits to Earth, checking on events and relaying them back to Robert.

CHAPTER FIFTEEN

Earth Year 1973

(I think it's time for my return to Earth.) Robert told Jal-sa-Lem and Cre-na-Tal. (Our work on terraforming is coming along well, but for it to work, we are going to need access to a rocket ship. According to Mar-wa-Len, there is a rocket launching station in a place called Houston Texas. They have launched almost 40 rockets into space since opening in 1965.)

(Our people will certainly miss you here Robert.) Thought Jal-sa-Lem. (You've have become a treasured member of our society.)

(Thank you. I feel the same towards all of you. However, if I am to continue helping you, I must return to Earth to gather the necessary people and resources.)

(So what is your plan?) Asked Jal-sa-Lem.

(I'll settle in the Houston Texas area and with your financial help, I plan on attending school there to get my degrees in various sciences. I'm sure I'll do well seeing as I could probably teach the classes thanks to you. But this will validate me in the eyes of everyone there.)

(Sounds good. While you are doing that, we will continue our research.) Thought Cre-na-Tal.

(Alright, take me back please. I am anxious to see the changes on Earth.) Thought Robert. (Mar-wa-Len has shared so many stories about the changes on Earth, I'm thinking I won't even recognize my home planet!)

Jal-sa-Lem replied, (After everything you have seen here and everything you have learned, I believe you'll make the adjustment just fine.)

(I appreciate your confidence.) Thought Robert. (Lets go and see if you are correct!)

Circling around the Earth, Jal-sa-Lem and Robert looked down on the blue ball hanging in space.

Robert said, "I just realized, I'm truly alone now. Everyone I knew when I left Earth is dead and gone. I'll need to re-build my network of Protectors."

"True. Rosalind and Brian maintained the network for a while, but it was difficult for them to trust others with the truth. It hasn't been an issue, so don't worry about that." Said Jal-sa-Lem.

"That's fine, and I understand the time displacement now, but part of me still thought I'd come back to the people I knew." Robert shook his head. "Crazy, right?"

"Not at all my friend. I understand completely." Replied Jal-sa-Lem.

"Well." Said Robert. "I'm starting fresh, I guess I should choose a new name as well. How about, Mitchell Church?"

"That sounds like a fine American name and suits you well." Agreed Jal-sa-Lem.

"Alright then. Take me down to my new home."

CHAPTER SIXTEEN

Rice University

Houston, Texas

Earth Year 1989

"Well Mr. Church, This is getting repetitive isn't it?" Smiled Dr. Eric George, President of Rice University. "What is this now, your fifth degree?"

"What can I say, I love to learn and I truly feel at home here at Rice." Replied Mitchell.

"Rice is your home for as long as you like, but at some point don't you want to use all of this knowledge you've accumulated?"

"Certainly I do." Mitchell replied. "I have one more degree I want to obtain. Then I'll look at what to do with them. I'm thinking about starting a tech company. I've got some ideas I want to try."

"I look forward to seeing great things coming out of any company you start." Said President George.

"Thank you, sir. How does Tomorrow Tech sound?"

"Impressive Mitchell, very impressive." Smiled Dr. George.

CHAPTER SEVENTEEN

Earth Year 2017

De Gelderlander newsroom

Nijmegen, Gelderland, Netherlands

Editor-in-Chief Simon Van den Berg was having a normal day. In other words, the news room was loud and hectic. Printing deadline was fast approaching, and everyone was trying to complete their articles before Simon came after them. "Come on people!" he yelled. "Papers don't write themselves! And don't try to give me any crap stories!"

As he passed the desk of his star reporter Maarten Jansen, he asked, "What have you got for me? Please make it good!"

Jansen answered, "Crazy story about some professor over at the university who's going looking for the Loch Ness Monster."

Simon stopped in his tracks. As a member of the Protectors, he didn't often get the opportunity to contribute to the cause, but this might be his chance.

"What do you mean? How?" he asked.

Jansen replied, "I think she's bonkers, but she said she can prove Nessie's existence by testing the water for the monster's DNA."

"Print me a copy of that, it sounds interesting." Said Simon.

Later in his office Simon sent a text to Clarence. 'Need to talk to Mr. Church. Hunters heading to Scotland'

Within the hour, his cell rang. "Hello Sir." He answered. "Thanks for calling."

"I don't really have a choice." Said Mitchell. "Your message was quite compelling. Give me the story."

Van den Berg explained. "So, there's a professor over here looking for funding to collect water samples of Loch Ness. Thinks she'll find DNA traces of Nessie in the water."

"Hmm." Mitchell said. "She needs funding. I might be interested in funding an expedition to my home country. Of course, for that kind of money I'll expect my people to be involved."

Van den Berg asked, "Would you like me to contact her and set up a meeting?"

"Yes, please Simon. Let her know I saw the story and called you."

TOMMOROW TECH
INC. HEADQUARTERS
OFFICE OF FOUNDER AND PRESIDENT
MITCHELL CHURCH

A few days later, Mitchell received a call from Utrecht University in the Netherlands.

"Mr. Church? This is Professor Alexandra De Vries. I understand you are interested in my research."

"Hello Professor! Yes, I am. My friend Simon told me about what you are proposing, and I think it's a fascinating idea. If you still need financing, I'll be glad to meet with you and discuss details."

Professor De Vries said, "Wait a moment sir. Not to be rude, I certainly could use a grant from you, but I need to know that you are truly interested in this project. My work isn't a joke and I don't take kindly to being laughed at."

"Let me assure you doctor; I'm not laughing at you. I'm originally from Scotland and I'm a believer in Nessie. If we can prove her existence, I will die a happy man."

Professor De Vries said, "Well then, we should work together. When can we meet?"

"As it happens, I'll be in the Netherlands next week for some meetings. I'll put you in touch with my assistant Clarence and you two can work out the scheduling."

"Sounds great." Said De Vries. "I look forward to his call. Good-bye and thanks. This means a lot to me."

Mitchell hung up and paged Clarence. "My friend, I have a lot for you to do."

Clarence laughed. "How is today different than any other sir?"

Mitchell chuckled. "I do keep you hopping, don't I? Maybe it's time to retire."

"No offense intended sir, but I can't retire. I don't know how you survived the last 400 plus years without me!"

Mitchell said, "Actually I meant me, but you are correct. I couldn't keep up with all the technology nowadays without you. My life back in Scotland was so much simpler. Oh, I do so miss those long-lost days."

Clarence leaned in and said, "Just think sir. Because of you, an entire race of beings has been saved from extinction. Just because it's not well known doesn't mean you aren't a hero."

"Hero? I don't know about that. I'm glad I was there to meet Jal-sa-Lem. My life was given meaning that day. No, I'm not a hero, I'm a grateful man."

"Either way sir, you've done a great thing and I'm sure the Tacharan think you are a hero. Now, what's next? What do you need me to do with the nice doctor?"

Mitchell outlined his plan to Clarence. "We need credentials forged for Rosalind and Brian. She is now a Scottish historian and botanist. Well respected, but obscure, hard to trace. Brian is a top researcher at our think tank in New Zealand. Very Top Secret hush-hush. Contact Constable Daniels and Captain Andrews. We will need all of them in on this. Professor De Vries project is too big, and we have a lot of bases to cover. If she is successful, she will harm all of our work."

Clarence said, "Well, I'm glad I've got a free moment to take care of this for you. I'll get right to it. Anything else?"

"Yes." Said Mitchell. "Set up a meeting next week for me with the good professor. I need to let her know my requirements for letting her spend my money."

"You think she'll go along with all of this? You're basically hi-jacking her project."

"Hi-jacking? How crude!" said Mitchell with a grin. "I'm facilitating with money and experienced personnel her dream of proving the existence of a unique life form. How can she not be thrilled?"

Nine Days Later

"What!? Shouted Dr. De Vries.

"Now Professor, let's talk this out as rational adults." Said Mitchell.

"Rational? Are you kidding me? You basically are trying to buy my idea out from under me!" exclaimed De Vries. "I won't stand for this. I thank you for coming all this way, but you might as well go home. I'll find my funding elsewhere!"

"Look, I'm as interested in finding Nessie as you are. This is completely your idea, your project, and your findings. I want no part of the credit or publicity. I'm willing to put up hundreds of thousands of dollars to make this a reality. I don't think it unreasonable to have a few of my people along to help you. You are fully in charge of the works. You must admit that an undertaking of this magnitude requires many hands. I have experienced professionals ready to help you succeed. Don't throw away this opportunity to prove your theory professor."

"Your people will do as I say, follow my lead in all matters?" asked De Vries.

"Completely, you have my word." Said Mitchell. "As of right now, they are not my people, they are yours."

"Well, maybe I was a bit hasty. Just that I've seen colleagues lose their research, and I won't let that happen to me."

"No doctor, I assure you that is not what is happening here." Said Mitchell. "I am going to do everything in my power to see you succeed in this endeavor."

"I apologize for my rudeness Mr. Church and I hope you can accept that. If you are still on board, let's make this happen."

"Sounds good." Said Mitchell. "Anytime you feel things aren't going right, you be sure to tell me. Agreed?"

"Thank you, Mr. Church. I feel much better now."

"Call me Mitchell please.   We're friends now!"

"And you can call me Alex, all of my friends do." Said De Vries.

Loch Ness, Scotland

Two weeks later

Alex and Mitchell stood on the banks of Loch Ness. The cool July breeze was blowing at 64 degrees Fahrenheit. Quite warm for the area, but Mitchell was still bundled up. "You'd think I would be ok with this weather, but all these years in Texas has really thinned my blood. Hard to tell I grew up right around here, isn't it?"

Alex laughed, "This is perfect weather where I'm from! Plus, it's a dry season, so we don't have the wet air cutting into us. You need to toughen up!"

Mitchell chuckled, "Yes ma'am! I'll work on it. In the meantime, everything is falling into place very nicely."

"I feel like I owe you another apology" said Alex. "Rosalind, Brian, and Captain Andrews are doing an amazing job collecting the samples. At this rate, we will be done ahead of schedule and testing can begin in my lab."

"No apologies necessary Alex. You had every right to be defensive of your idea and project. I'm just glad we could straighten it out and work together."

"Me too." Said Alex. "By the way, where are Rosalind and Brian?"

"Oh." said Mitchell. "Since we are so far ahead of projection, I gave them the day off for sightseeing. It's been awhile since Brian has been to Scotland and I thought they both could use the break. Chief Daniels should be along any time now to pick up the samples we have ready."

Inwardly, Mitchell felt a pang of regret for lying to Alex. She was a dedicated, hardworking scientist, but his duty to protect the Tacharan outweighed any other consideration.

Meanwhile on Loch Lomond

Rosalind, Brian, and Captain Andrews were enjoying the brisk weather on the loch.

"Ya canna find a more beautiful time to boat on Loch Lomond than now!" said Andrews. "Besides Loch Ness, these are my favorite waters!"

"It is lovely." agreed Rosalind, "but we aren't here for sightseeing Michael."

"True Rosalind, but it doesn't hurt to admire the scenery." Said Brian. "I don't get to see Scotland very often. I for one am thoroughly enjoying the day!"

"Alright boys! Its two against one, I give!" Rosalind joked. "Enjoy your weather while I get the work done."

"I don't see why we can't just fill a bucket of water and take it back." Said Andrews. "What's the big deal?"

"The 'big deal' is that Mr. Church said to follow the same protocol that we are following at Loch Ness." Said Brian. "That way he can honestly say that all protocols were followed to the letter when the study goes south, and they don't find anything."

"Besides," Rosalind jabbed, "It gives you more time to enjoy your loch Mr. Andrews!"

"True true Rosalind. Go collect your samples and I'll cruise us around to the map points laid out for us." Agreed Michael.

Fort Augustus Police Station

Fort William Road

Boleshine and Abertarff parish

Southwest end of Loch Ness

Scottish Highlands, Scotland.

Population: less than 637

Chief Constable Ian Daniels said, "I understand Clarence. I'll take care of it just as Mr. Church wants. "No one here will be the wiser."

Daniels hung up the phone and called out to Sergeant Fleming. "Aubrey! We are going to be using the north cells to safeguard some water samples from Loch Ness for a scientific research project. Have them cleared out please."

"Yes Sir" said Aubrey. "I'll have it done straight away. When will the samples arrive?" She asked.

Daniels answered, "They're being collected as we speak, and so over the next few days I'll be going up to the researchers' camp to pick up the samples. Not sure how many samples are coming, so make sure both cells are empty. They need to be secure so that no one tampers with them."

"Not a problem Sir. I don't think we are expecting any crime waves here, so I'm sure we can spare two cells." Aubrey smiled.

"Thanks." Said Daniels. "I'm going to head over there now to check on the progress. Hold down the fort for me 'till I get back."

Daniels grabbed his jacket and hat as he went out to his patrol car. It was just a quick 20 minute trip up the A82 to meet up with Mitchell at his camp at Urquhart Castle.

As he arrived, Daniels saw Mr. Church walking along the loch with Dr. De Vries. He sounded his car horn and waved to them.

"Ah here is Constable Daniels now." Said Mitchell.

"And we do trust him to treat the samples carefully, yes?" Questioned Alex for the umpteenth time.

Mitchell sighed. "Yes doctor we do. He has been a family friend for as long as I can remember and a Nessie believer. He wants your research to prove her existence too."

"Hello!" Called Daniels. "Are the samples ready to go?"

"Yes." Said Mitchell. "All carefully packaged and ready for your safekeeping. At the pace we are going, we should be done and out of your way in two more days."

"No worries at all sir." Said Daniels. "Sergeant Fleming has the cells cleared and ready for you."

"I would like to accompany the samples back to your station and see to their safety myself." Said Alex.

"There's no need ma'am. We will take good care of them for you." Daniels tried to assure.

"That's Doctor, not ma'am, and I really insist." Alex replied hotly.

"Why don't we all go and see the station, hmm?" Asked Mitchell diffusing the situation. "It's been awhile since I've been to Fort Augustus and I seem to recall the restaurant at the castle was quite excellent, so lunch is on me!"

"Sounds good sir." Answered Daniels. "Let's load up and go. I for one am getting hungry!"

"Good, lets." Agreed Alex.

So after loading the water samples and leaving word for Rosalind and Brian, the trio headed back down the highway to Fort Augustus. Since Daniels wouldn't be returning right away to the camp, Mitchell and Alex followed him in their car. This gave Daniels the chance to call Aubrey to warn her.

"The doctors a bit on the fussy side so please make double sure we are spot on for her."

"Yes sir." Said Aubrey. "I'll be ready for her."

Arriving at the station, they were met by Sergeant Fleming at the door.

"Welcome to the Fort Augustus Police Station Dr. De Vries, Mr. Church. I am Sergeant Aubrey Fleming. Anything you need or want, I will be happy to help you."

Mitchell shook her hand and said, "Thank you sergeant. It's a pleasure to meet you. Constable Daniels has told me much about you. All good I assure you."

Alex stepped forward and said, "Sergeant, will you show us where my samples will be safeguarded please?"

"Yes of course doctor. Everyone, right this way please." Replied Aubrey. As Alex walked past her, Aubrey wagged her eyebrows at Daniels.

Inside the station, Alex scrutinized every detail. Aubrey led them to the cells she had prepared and explained what had been done.

"As you can see," She began. "The cots have been removed and this shelving brought in to safely store your samples."

"And who has access to these cells?" Asked Alex.

Daniels replied, "There are six of us here on the force. All have access to the keys, however, the north cells are keyed differently than the south cells, so for the time being only Sergeant Fleming and I have the keys to these cells. Additionally there are always two of us on duty here at all times and to get to these cells you must pass through three other locked doors as you saw."

"Are you comfortable with the arrangements Alex?" Asked Mitchell.

"I think so." She replied. "I'm sorry if I've rubbed any of you the wrong way. I just have so much riding on this."

"No apologies needed." Said Mitchell. "I'm sure everyone understands."

Daniels and Fleming nodded their agreement and Alex sighed her relief.

"Now!" said Mitchell. "Enough of this talk. Let's get those samples in here and go eat! I'm famished!"

Everyone pitched in and brought the samples in while Alex shelved and labeled them. When they were done, Daniels locked the heavy metal door with a loud clang.

"No one is touching your waters until you say so doctor."

"Thanks constable, I appreciate this."

"Aubrey, you're on guard duty. We're going for lunch. I'll bring you back some food. Shepherd's Pie or fish and chips?"

"You know I can never turn down a good shepherd's pie. Especially if you include some sticky pudding. Please?"

"I'll make sure he doesn't forget." Said Alex with a grin.

"Thank you!" replied Aubrey.

Over lunch Mitchell and Daniels kept the conversation light and centered on Alex to keep her mind away from the project.

Daniels asked, "So tell me about yourself. I've never been to the Netherlands; I hear it's quite beautiful."

"Oh it is." Alex agreed. My university is one of the oldest in the Netherlands dating back to 1636. We've had a dozen Nobel Prize recipients including Wilhelm Rontgen, the Father of Radiology. We have 21 museums, nine art galleries, and the best restaurants anywhere!"

"Well." Said Daniels, "After this project is done, maybe I'll take a holiday and go there. It sounds quite lovely!"

"Let me know, I'll be your tour guide if you want." Alex blushed as she realized what she said.

Daniels smiled, "I'd like that very much."

Mitchell cleared his throat and said, "I'm full and in need of some rest. Let's order Aubrey's food

171

and I'll settle up the bill. Ian, maybe Alex would like to tour the castle?"

"I would actually." Said Alex. "Do you have the time?"

"I'm the boss, so I think so." Smiled Daniels. "I'll see that she makes it home sir. Do you mind dropping Aubrey's meal off to her?"

"Not at all!" Mitchell laughed and said good-bye. On the way out he paid the waiter and left a generous tip.

Getting into his car, Mitchell called Clarence.

Clarence answered, "Yes sir. How are we doing with Dr. De Vries?"

"She has been skeptical at every step but I think we are good for now. The sooner we finish this the better. Contact Ros and Brian and let them know I want the timetable upped. Let's wrap this phase up ASAP."

"I will inform them sir." Replied Clarence.

"Alright," Said Rosalind. "You heard the man. Our two days are now one. No more sightseeing Michael let's get this done."

Twenty-eight hours later, Daniels arrived at Urquhart Castle to retrieve the final samples.

"Hello." Said Alex. "Do you know the plan from here?" She asked of Daniels.

"I'll bring these over to the station. Rosalind and Brian will meet me there to finish cataloguing and packing them for shipment. Mr. Church has arranged for a courier to escort the samples to the Inverness Airport where he has one of his private jets waiting to take them to Schiphol Amsterdam. They will then transfer to another courier and be delivered to Utrecht University for you."

"When is the courier picking them up from you?" She asked.

"9am tomorrow morning." Daniels answered.

"Good. Have coffee ready. I'll be at your station at 8am to look over the packing. I will be escorting the samples back to my lab."

Mitchell said, "I've covered all the bases Alex. I thought you might want to stay in Scotland for a couple extra days. You haven't had a chance to see anything really."

"No. I won't be able to enjoy myself if I don't see my samples safely home and start the testing. If something happened in transit, I wouldn't forgive myself."

"I understand." Mitchell took out his phone and called Clarence. "Hello. We are wrapping up here. Dr. De Vries will be accompanying the water samples from here to her lab. Please make all of the necessary arrangements for her. Thank you."

"Thanks Mitchell. This means a lot to me." She said.

"I know. Let's all hope the outcome is what we are looking for."

Daniels arrived at the police station and carried the last samples in. Aubrey greeted him and unlocked the cage.

"So we're almost done being a water storage tank, right?" she asked.

"As of tomorrow morning, yes." He replied. Just then, Rosalind and Brian came in.

"Hello!" called Brian. "Time to pack the water!"

"Have at it mate. "Said Daniels. "Aubrey, would you do us a favor and pop into town for some food? I think we will be at this for a while and I'm getting hungry."

"No problem sir." She replied. "Anything in particular?"

"Naw. Here's my card. Don't go too crazy but get enough for four people to eat a couple meals please. And take your time, no rush."

Aubrey left and Daniels turned to Brian.

"Do you have the other samples?"

"Yes. All ready to bring in." Brian replied.

"Alright. Let's bring them in and make the exchange before Aubrey returns. Ros, Brian and I

175

will move the boxes if you can start the packing and labeling."

"Sounds good." Said Rosalind. "I'll get to it as soon as you bring in the first box."

The men made quick work of the swap and Ros was labeling her third box when Aubrey returned with the food.

"Ah good!" exclaimed Daniels. "Break time!"

The four of them ate well and talked between bites about the project. Since Aubrey wasn't a Protector. The others were careful about what they said.

"A little excitement is nice, but it will be good to get back to normal." Said Daniels.

"Agreed." Said Aubrey. "It will be interesting to see the results. This area will explode if they actually find something."

"Well we know that's not happening, right?" Asked Brian. "I mean, come on! It's fun to pretend there's a monster, but no one here really believes it right?"

Aubrey said, "I don't know. It's kind of hard not to with so many sightings. It does seem far-fetched though. However, my kid sister Maddie swears she saw Nessie along with her friends one evening near Urquhart."

"As far as I'm concerned, until I see it, it doesn't exist." Stated Daniels. "How about you Ros?"

"'There are more things in heaven and earth, Horatio, then are dreamt of in your philosophy.' At least according to Mr. Shakespeare. I don't believe so no, but I certainly don't pretend to know everything. I guess I agree with Daniels. Show it to me."

"Well we will never know if we don't finish packing up the samples for shipping." Said Daniels. "So let's get back to work."

They all pitched in and finished up the labeling. When they were finished, it was close to dawn.

Daniels bid them all good-bye and went to rest on the couch he had in his office.

"I can take watch if you want Ian." Said Aubrey.

"I'm fine thanks." He replied. "Besides, you need rest too and Dr. De Vries will be here in a few hours to meet the courier."

"Alright, try to get some rest then and I'll see you later." Said Aubrey as she left.

True to her word, Alex was there at the stroke of eight. Daniels woke as Alex called out to him.

"Constable Daniels! Are you here?" She said.

"Ah! Yes!" He cleared his throat. "I'm in here. Just a minute."

He walked out of his office to find Alex with her bags waiting by the locked door leading to the north cells.

"I'm anxious to check my samples and you said you would have coffee ready when I got here!" she joked with him.

"So sorry! I overslept. We were at it quite late last night. Just laid down about 4am." He replied.

"Oh you poor dear! Why don't I run into town and get us some coffee and breakfast then? You certainly could use it as much as me." She offered.

"That is a splendid idea, but I'll go while you start looking over your boxes. That way we kill two birds with one stone. I won't be long."

With that, he opened up the doors and cells for Alex and headed out.

She proceeded to look over the boxes and labels to make sure nothing was missed or out of place. As far as she could see, there wasn't anything missed. As she returned to the front office, Daniels returned.

"Well, how'd we do?" He asked.

"Everything looks perfect!" Alex replied. "I'm just such a worrier and planner."

"Nothing wrong with that." Assured Daniels. "If it weren't for people like you, people like me would be in a mess!"

Just then the courier arrived. Between the three of them, they checked off and moved the boxes to the delivery van.

"Tell me again your name please?" Alex asked of the courier.

"Hawkes ma'am, Albert Hawkes. Everyone just calls me Hawkes."

"Alright then Hawkes. Give me a few moments and then we will be on our way." She said.

Hawkes replied, "Very good ma'am." as he left.

"Well this is it." Alex said. "Again, I truly appreciate all you've done for me. I hope to repay you soon."

"I'll be seeing you and taking you up on that tour guide offer." He smiled.

The ride to the airport was without incident and the exchange from van to airplane went as planned.

Within a couple of hours of leaving Fort Augustus, Alex was in the air headed home.

TOMORROW TECH INC. HEADQUARTERS

Two Days Later

Office of Dr. Patricia Martinez

Lead Scientist at T.T.I. and a Protector

"How are we doing Dr. Martinez?" Asked Mitchell.

"On schedule sir." She replied. "The boxes arrived this morning from Scotland, and we are sorting them out now."

"Good!" Mitchell smiled. "You have the genetic samples that Jal-sa-Lem gave us to compare?"

"Yes sir. I've kept them safeguarded waiting for this testing."

"Excellent. Contact me the moment you have results, one way or the other."

"Will do sir." Patricia replied.

CHAPTER EIGHTEEN

UTRECHT UNIVERSITY

THE NETHERLANDS

"Are we ready to begin testing?" Asked Alex. She had her entire team assembled before her as well as some of the other faculty of the sciences departments to observe.

"Yes Doctor De Vries." Answered her lead assistant Victor. "The samples are split up into 20 units representing the various locations they were collected from around Loch Ness. Each team has all known DNA markers in their computers for comparison as they have findings."

"Very good!" Alex nodded. She addressed the gathered researchers. "You all know what this will mean to me, the university, Scotland, and the world if we can identify just one strand of unknown DNA from these waters. We will all be remembered for making one of the greatest discoveries of our lifetime. Take your time, be diligent in your work. No matter what time of the day or night, if anything looks remotely different, I expect to be contacted immediately. Good luck to you all and Godspeed. Now, let's find Nessie!"

A cheer went up from the room as Alex went out of the lab to her office three doors down the hall. She needed to leave the lab before someone noticed how badly her hands were shaking. In her office she sat down on her couch and, not meaning too, fell into a much needed sleep.

TOMORROW TECH INC. HEADQUARTERS
Sub-Basement Laboratory

"Sir," Said Patricia over the phone. "You may wish to meet me in the lab."

"On my way." Said Mitchell. "Clarence!" he called out the door, "Let's go!"

Clarence entered and asked, "Dr. Martinez?"

"Yes and she sounded happy. Not sure if that means 'happy she found something' or 'happy she didn't'. We will just need to wait and find out."

Taking his express elevator from his office to the sub-basement lab, Mitchell along with Clarence rode in silence, each lost in their own thoughts.

When the doors opened, Dr. Martinez was standing there waiting for them.

"Hello Clarence, Mr. Mitchell. Welcome! I have some interesting results for you."

"Oh my god Patricia! Just spill it! Did you find Tacharan DNA in the water or not?" Said Mitchell.

"Well, I wanted to be a bit more dramatic, but, yes we did!" smiled Dr. Martinez. "It matched perfectly with Jal-sa-Lems cells. "If you hadn't intervened, the world would know that Loch Ness is no joke."

Mitchell let out a huge sigh. "Good lord that was a close one. If Simon had not caught the story and contacted me, Alex would have ruined everything I've tried so hard to protect. I've got to speak with Cre-na-Tal. We must perfect the terraforming device and settle this once and for all! Dr. Martinez, you have all of my research along with Cre-na-Tals. Get everyone we can trust on this immediately. All other projects are on hold indefinitely until we have this settled!"

"Yes Sir Mr. Church. It will be done." She replied.

"Good. I want continuous updates on my desk. Now get to it!"

UTRECHT UNIVERSITY
THE NETHERLANDS

"So where are you going?" Asked Victor.

"Oh I don't know," replied Alex. "Somewhere warm I think. I've had enough of cold for a while. I hear Puerto Rico is a wonderful island. Maybe I'll head there."

"You don't have to leave." Said Victor. "The university isn't firing you."

"I know Victor, but I need a break. I really was expecting to find something; you know?" She shook her head. "I'll tell you something Victor that I haven't told anyone else. While I was at Loch Ness collecting the samples. One night, I looked out at the water and I swear I saw her."

"Who?" asked Victor.

"Who else? Nessie!" Alex said. "Just as plain as I see you. Her head lifted out of the water and she turned towards me and look me dead in the eye. It was over in a second, but I'm sure of what I saw."

"Well why didn't you say something? You need to let people know so we can try again!"

Alex laughed. "No Victor. I can't tell anyone! Don't you see? They will all think I'm lying to support my theory! I'm in a no win scenario. If I tell, I'm a liar. If I don't tell, it's going to drive me crazy! That's why I just need to get away and forget all of this mess!"

Victor bowed his head and said, "I'm so sorry. I wish I could help you."

"Don't worry about me." Alex said. "Go do something brilliant and thank me when you get an award. That will make me feel better."

CHAPTER NINETEEN

TOMORROW TECH INC. HEADQUARTERS

Patricia was falling asleep on her desk when the simulation alarm went off for the 112th attempt. Her head slipped off her hand and almost slammed into the desktop when she caught herself. She reached over and stopped the blaring sound coming from her computer.

Talking to herself, she said, 'Let's see where we went wrong this time Patricia.'

She stood up, stretched her back and walked over to the isolation chamber where the testing was taking place. She sighed, looked up from her clipboard, and stared into the chamber. Dropping her clipboard, she grabbed for the intercom switch besides her.

"Mitchell!" She screamed. "We've done it! Get down here!"

Mitchell and Clarence raced for the elevator that would take them down to the sub-basement. The slow ride seemed to taunt them as it took its time.

Mitchell turned to Clarence and asked, "Well? What do you think we will find?"

"No use speculating sir, we are here!" Answered Clarence.

At that, the elevator doors opened and they were greeted by Dr. Martinez. Her smile looked as if it would split her face.

"I'm playing 1-1-2 in the Pick Three Lottery tonight! Attempt 112 paid off for us. The plants are growing and the isolation chamber is turning into a giant terrarium!" Exclaimed Dr. Martinez.

The trio rushed over to the chamber and peered through the thick glass wall. The condensation on the window made visibility difficult, but not impossible. Patricia was correct, the once lifeless room was now thriving. Mitchell swore he could actually see the plants growing.

"This is fantastic doctor! Congratulations!" He said.

"I'm not alone in this sir. You and Cre-na-Tal and all the others deserve credit as well. I'm thrilled to be a part of this."

"Clarence, send word to Jal-sa-Lem and Cre-na-Tal right away. Tell them to transport over here as soon as they can."

"I'm on it sir." Clarence replied.

"Remarkable!" Cried Cre-na-Tal as she stepped into the reformed chamber. "Truly a miracle!"

Jal-sa-Lem agreed, "Yes, this is astounding! Congratulations to all of you. Phase one is now complete, where are we on Phase two and three?"

"Phase two, finding a suitable planet is complete as well. Phase three is about to begin. I signed a contract yesterday with Space X to build our rocket and Houston Control will facilitate the launch!" Answered Mitchell.

Jal-sa-Lem turned to Cre-na-Tal and said, "Just think my friend. Soon we will have a true home again. We will be able to walk and swim and live under our own sun. Our young won't live in darkness anymore!"

Cre-na-Tal nodded. "I hope I am still alive when that dream is reality. I fear that won't be the case. As happy as I am now, I feel my life force slipping away. But I am not sad. I am prepared and look forward to seeing Mak-na-Tal again."

Mitchell responded, "Please don't speak like this! You above all Tacharan need to see this to fruition! You deserve to walk, not in a simulation chamber, but across a real landscape that you helped create!"

"Alright Mitchell. For your sake, I will strive to continue this existence until our new home is complete." Cre-na-Tal agreed.

CHAPTER TWENTY

JOHNSON SPACE CENTER

HOUSTON TEXAS

Countdown to launch of Mission Tacharan

Mission Date: October 29th, 2020

'T-minus 5 minutes and counting' announced the computer countdown clock.

Mission Analyst Thompson said, "Well Mr. Church, are you excited for the launch?"

"Of course I am! This is a huge step for us and humanity. Just think about it. In less than 5 minutes, that rocket is going to launch, go to Alpha and turn that bleak and barren planet into a lush garden that can support human life! How can you not be excited about that?" Mitchell asked.

"Well we are all proud to be a part of your project sir. Good luck!" Wished Thompson.

'Orbiter transfers from ground to internal power T-minus 50 seconds'

"Thank you." said Mitchell.

In the back of his mind he knew of course that the mission would not be a success to the rest of the world. For him it would be a remarkable realization of a centuries old dream, but in the eyes of the world it would be a colossal failure.

'Ground launch sequencer is go for auto sequence start T-minus 31 seconds'

Thompson leaned across his workstation, "Can I ask some other questions sir?"

"Yes, after the launch." Mitchell replied. "Let's watch."

'Activate launch pad sound suppression system T-minus 16 seconds

Activate main engine hydrogen burnoff system T-minus 10 seconds

194

__Main engine start T-minus 6.6 seconds__

__T-minus zero seconds__

__Solid rocket booster ignition and liftoff!__

__We have lift off!__

__Successful launch of Tacharan I. On course to NGC 2685.'__

Everyone in Mission Control let out a collective breath, applauded and cheered.

"Beautiful launch!" said NASA Administrator Collins. "What's next for your team Mitchell?"

"If this proves successful," said Mitchell, "we can terraform the moon and settle people there. We can move humanity out into the cosmos and explore!"

"Sir, if I may ask, why didn't we just attempt this with our moon? It's so much closer it would have cost less and we could observe it much easier."

"You are correct Thompson but think what could happen if something went wrong with the experiment and Earth was threatened by it. No, I wouldn't be able to live with myself if that happened. If we are successful with Alpha, the moon will be next."

'Secondary thrusters engaged

Course corrections entered'

"So" Asked Thompson, "How long do we wait for the celebration?"

"We still have a week to reach Alpha." said Mitchell. "With no complications, within three weeks after that, we should have an Earth Two on our hands."

"How soon can we launch people to Alpha?"

"Well, I'd say in about two weeks. That gives us time to reach Alpha, and observe positive changes taking place. Then by the time our colony ship arrives there, the planet should be ready to accept and support our people." Said Mitchell.

"Director!" called out a technician, "Somethings gone wrong. Tacharan I is way off course and not accepting corrections."

Mitchell demanded, "Collins, do something! That ship cost me a fortune!"

"We've got this Mr. Mitchell. Now stand aside please and let us work!" ordered Collins.

Collins asked, "What is the ships heading now?"

Thompson replied, "She's on a trajectory to impact in the constellation Ursa Major Sir."

"That's a 45-degree deviation Collins!" said Mitchell. "What is wrong with your people?"

"It looks like a programming error sir." Said Thompson. "Apparently our program was overwritten by an outside source."

"Espionage?" questioned Collins. "Who wouldn't want something like this to work?"

"Obviously you don't know your staff as well as you thought Collins. My lawyers will be in touch if that ship isn't redirected and on Alpha in one week." Mitchell said as he left the building.

Upon reaching his car, Mitchell called Clarence. "Hello my friend. It seems you've been busy."

"Yes sir" Said Clarence. "All is going according to your plan. The ship will disappear from their radar within a day, seemingly going straight for Ursa Major and one of its suns. Once contact is lost, onboard systems will boot up and redirect the ship to *Centaurus A NGC 5128*. By then no one will be watching for a 'destroyed' ship."

"Excellent work Clarence. Give yourself a raise." Joked Mitchell.

"I already did Sir. Thank you. You are most generous." Said Clarence as he hung up the phone.

Mitchell shook his head and laughed as he drove towards home.

(Mar-wa-Len! Can you hear me?) Thought Mitchell (Our plan is on course!)

(That's wonderful my friend! You have done a great thing for my people!)

(We're not done yet. We still need the terraforming to go right, your people need to set up the tubes to get there, so many things could go wrong.) Mitchell thought.

(I am confident in your science along with ours. This will work and the Tacharan can once again flourish in a real home. We are all quite excited! Cre-na-Tal sends you her congratulations and thanks as well.)

(Well control yourselves for a couple of weeks and we will see what happens. I'll see you back at T.T.I.)

THE NEXT DAY

"Well Collins?" demanded Mitchell. "Where's my ship!?"

Collins replied, "Mr. Church, I regret to inform you that at 12:47PM today, Tacharan I disappeared from our radar and we have been unable to re-establish contact or control. Our best guess estimates are that the ship is on a collision course for Messier 97 in the Owl Nebula and should impact in 72 hours."

"TWO BILLION DOLLARS COLLINS!! You lost two billion dollars of my money and that's all you can tell me?"

"I am sorry sir." Apologized Collins. "My team and I take errors very personally as well. My only comfort is that no one was on the ship. I can tell you that we have identified a signal trace from an outside source at seven minutes from launch."

"Now you are giving me factual information we can use." Said Mitchell. "Where did that signal originate?"

"We are still following the trail, and believe me when I say, not only are our best people on this, but we won't stop investigating until we know who is responsible. Our search so far has found out that the signal was pinged through three separate platforms. The last signal we have tracked originated in Canada, but we don't believe that is the final link."

"I want all of your data sent to my assistant Clarence. I'll have my people track this as well." Said Mitchell. "I also highly suggest you work on better securing your systems against a future incident like this."

"We are looking at how they got in sir, but quite honestly it's baffling. It's as if they were able to destroy our firewalls from within. The tech used for this is at least a decade beyond us. Truly it's a bit frightening." Said Collins.

"I'll expect Clarence to have that data soon and for you to keep me updated with any developments." Said Mitchell as he disconnected the call.

Mitchell turned to Clarence and asked, "Are they going to find you at the end of their trail?"

"Not possible." Deflected Clarence. "The Tacharan tech I employed is unbreakable with earth tech. They have two more signal sources to find. The next one is in Russia, and the final one is in China. They will of course petition the governments there for information, but that's not going to happen. Even if they cooperated, there's nothing to find which will further look like they don't want to help."

"Very devious Clarence! Once again I'm glad you are on my side!" said Mitchell. "You know, When James Dunlop first discovered NGC 5128 from his home in Australia, he probably wondered if there was life on one of the planets circling around those stars. In just a few weeks, there will be."

Clarence replied, "It's fitting that he was a Scottish astronomer. Sort of poetic don't you think?"

"Yes my friend it is." Smiled Mitchell.

ONE WEEK LATER

CENTAURUS CONSTELLATION

The fifth brightest galaxy in the night sky, the nearest giant galaxy to the Milky Way.

Coordinates: 13h 25m 27.6s (right ascension)

-43°01'09" (declination)

NEW DESIGNATION: MOTHAN II

Tacharan I circled the grey ball hanging in the unexplored region of space. In its present condition, nothing could survive even 30 seconds on the planet's surface.

The ships onboard systems identified its final destination had been accomplished and activated her deployment protocol. 21 bay doors opened along the outer hull as the launch countdown began. Since Mothan II was approximately the same size as Earth, and at a speed of 17,500 miles per hour, it would take Tacharan I ninety minutes to circle the planet. One satellite would launch every four and a half minutes along the equator and land on the planet's surface. Three satellites would be directed to each of the polar icecaps as well. Once they were all in place, Tacharan I's systems would activate them, and the terraforming process would begin.

TOMORROW TECH INC.
HEADQUARTERS
Two Hours After Satellite Launch

"Well? Anything yet?" asked Mitchell pacing around his penthouse home.

"No sir." Replied Clarence. "Remember, Cre-na-Tal told us that the first signs would take approximately three hours and even then it would be slow progress for the first 24 hours."

Mitchell sighed, "I know, I know but I'm just so anxious to see this work!"

"I understand, but for someone your age, you should have more patience." Smiled Clarence.

"Look here Clarence, I'm not in the mood…."

"Sir! Look at this!" exclaimed Clarence.

"What is it?" Asked Mitchell.

"The atmospheric sensors, they're climbing! The icecaps have decreased in size by 50% which has released the CO2 trapped in the ice, giving us carbon dioxide and oxygen! It's working sir, its working!"

(Mar-wa-Len!)

(I know! Cre-na-Tal and I are watching as well. This is quite exciting for us all!) Thought Mar-wa-Len.

(Once the surface is ready, we can land the ship to activate the transportation tunnel aboard it.) Replied Mitchell.

(And then our people can begin settling our new home!) Added Cre-na-Tal. (If only Mak-na-Tal were here to share in this it would feel more complete.)

Lightening flashed, and the thunder crashed across the afternoon sky three days later. The new clean rain water fell on the saplings and the fresh grasses overlooking the green-blue valley lake. There were still areas of Mothan II that had not begun living yet, but in time they would.

Tacharan I lay next to the water's edge. To an outside observer, it would appear as a dead ship. On board though it was a different story. Automated systems were running at breakneck speeds to complete the connections to bring the transportation tunnel on line. Then, an alarm sounded signaling the activation of a transport being initiated from another tunnel. The lighting systems dimmed as the tunnel drew the power it needed to complete its task. The air was full of static and smelled like burnt wiring as the system began cycling down. Out of the tunnel stepped Mothan II's first citizen. Appropriately it was one of the planets creators, Cre-na-Tal. She had initially declined the honor feeling that there were more deserving amongst her people, but they had overwhelmingly over ruled her. As she opened the ships hatch and breathed in the newly created air on her new world, she thought back to her acceptance of this moment.

(Cre-na-Tal! Seriously? How can you not deserve this? If it weren't for you all these years, this project would never have been completed and our people would have lost all hope in having a new world.) Explained Kem-ka-Jen. (I may be the Chief Elder of Mothan, but Mothan II is more your world than mine!)

(I will accept this great honor) replied Cre-na-Tal. (But please, make no mistake. In the name of my Bond Mate Mak-na-Tal, this new world is all of ours equally. It would not honor his memory to think otherwise.)

(Believe me Cre-na-Tal, he along with all the others who perished in the Raider attack will be remembered and honored on Mothan II.)

(Speaking of the Raiders,) thought Cre-na-Tal. (I've been contemplating their situation. The reason they attacked us, and others, is that they no longer have a home planet. What I propose is that we share this tech with them. Let them create a new home to live on and then we all can go back to the days of peace when they were our friends and neighbors.)

(Outrageous! I would not expect this from you of all Tacharans. They murdered your Bond Mate and stole your planet. Now you would help them? They do not deserve your mercy Cre-na-Tal. It would be better if all their ships crashed into a star like the Earthlings believe our ship did.)

(No, maybe they do not deserve my mercy. But it is mine to give to whom I shall. Do you remember who the Raiders were before their planet died? The Síocháin, the peaceful ones. Yes, they created the disaster on their planet that destroyed it and turned them into the Raiders, but they weren't always that way. Perhaps we can lead them back. Perhaps they've paid for their mistakes. Perhaps it's time for them to rest.)

Kem-ka-Jen replied, (And perhaps they will take our tech and weaponize it to destroy even more civilizations. No. I cannot see us giving them this power.)

(You may be Chief Elder, but this cannot be your decision alone. I will speak to the assembly once we are all safely on Mothan II.)

Cre-na-Tal breathed a heavy sigh. The joy of seeing Mothan II was shadowed by the thoughts of Mak-na-Tal. (Oh, how I wish you were here with me.) Shaking her head, she thought, (But I know you wouldn't want me feeling sorry for myself when there is so much still to do. I will make you proud.)

She straightened her shoulders, strode out of the ship, and walked across the landscape of her new home. Her first duty was to check the soil, air and water for life sustaining viability and contaminates. She continued to admire the view while she collected her samples. Returning them to the ship, she placed them in the analyzers and sat back to wait on the results. She reached for the communicator and contacted Jal-sa-Lem.

"Jal-sa-Lem, this is Cre-na-Tal. Come in please." She radioed. The sound of her own voice sounded alien to her since she seldom spoke aloud.

"This is Jal-sa-Lem. I hear you. How is Mothan II?"

"Beautiful doesn't come close to describing her." She replied. "I'm running environmental samples now, however I believe everything will be well."

"Excellent! I am working with Mitchell gathering the animals. After your team joins you and you set up the other transportation tunnels, we can begin sending the animals to you."

"It will be wonderful to have a populated planet again." Cre-na-Tal exclaimed. "To hear birds singing will be a great joy for me."

"That is certainly one of the pleasures on being on Earth." Agreed Jal-sa-Lem.

TOMORROW TECH INC. HEADQUARTERS

Two Weeks Later

"Clarence, we are ready to begin transferring the animals to Mothan II. When can we expect their arrival?"

"Our friend at the zoo is working on that now. She has done an excellent job buying new animals, with your money of course, and hiding the paper trail. She was very happy to help with this project since she is the V.P. of Wildlife Conservation. Saving these beings from extinction is her passion."

Mitchell said, "I want the first ones delivered to our headquarters this weekend. The building will be empty of everyone except our circle and Jal-sa-Lem will be here to help with the transportation tunnel. Cre-na-Tal and her team are waiting on us."

Clarence replied, "I'll let Emeline know."

"I know this is important Clarence." Emeline said. "But I've got to take this easy. Not only is the rest of the admin team watching me, but I also have these animal rights activists monitoring my ever purchase. Even if I get past that, how am I going to explain away a couple thousand animals disappearing?"

"You have them all quarantined in the new building we donated to the zoo, yes?"

"Yes they are and I have people demanding to inspect them to ensure that we are following standards."

Clarence smiled. "Alright, I have a plan. Let them in to inspect. It will help our story. It's going to delay transport a week, but it will cover you with the inspectors, the activists, and your administration team. Mitchell won't like the delay, but it's the only viable way. Plus, you are going to be able to keep a couple hundred of the animals for your zoo!"

"Are you kidding Clarence?" Mitchell fumed. "There has got to be a better plan."

"Tell me what it is and I'll run with it. But unless you can, this is the plan. Sir."

"And you are sure the storm is coming here?"

"As sure as I can be sir. It is Hurricane Josephine and you know hurricanes and women can be fickle."

"This better work Clarence. The Tacharan are counting on us. I'll contact Cre-na-Tal and let her know."

"I understand the delay." Said Cre-na-Tal. "I want you people to be safe and we have waited a very long time for this. Another week or so will not harm us."

"Thanks my friend." Said Mitchell. "How's Mothan II looking?"

"She is absolutely beautiful." Exclaimed Cre-na-Tal. "More than I had hoped for. Our capital city is going up much faster than I expected and we are no longer sleeping in the ships."

"That's great!" Said Mitchell. "How are the farms doing?"

"The soil is very fertile and all of our crops are growing quite rapidly. Some of that may be a side benefit of the terraforming process. Either way, it is pleasing."

Mitchell replied, "I'm very happy to hear this. As soon as the animals arrive at my building, we will contact you to let you know."

"Thank you. Be safe." Cre-na-Tal said as she signed off.

KTEX NEWS AND WEATHER ALERT FOR TODAY NOVEMBER 29TH, 2020

HURRICANE JOSEPHINE EXPECTED TO HIT THE HOUSTON AREA THIS EVENING.

"It looks like you called it Clarence. That hurricane is going to hit about midnight tonight. We need to move!"

"Our timing has got to be perfect." Said Clarence. "The trucks are ready to move the animals. Everyone on site works for us. Emeline is there to oversee the transfers. Once the trucks are on the way, our team will collapse the building. With all of the chaos from the storm, everyone should believe that the majority of the animals escaped or were lost when the building came down. Emeline doctored the papers so that on record we only have half the number of animals we actually do."

"So now we wait and hope all goes as planned." Said Mitchell.

The winds were getting intense. Small branches and other debris were whipping through the air, and visibility was dropping quickly.

"Come on guys! Move! Move!" Called Emeline. "We need this done before the hurricane hits here!"

Her team picked up the pace and got the animals moved. Semi-truck "A" was aquatic animals. They were in tanks, so they would be good for a while. "R" truck was refrigerated. Penguins, seals, etc. They were cold, so they were happy. "B" truck were the birds. They were pretty upset with the move and the storm, so the plan was to get them relocated the fastest. The remaining six trucks were labeled "M" for mammals. They were almost as spooked as the birds, so they would be on Mothan II second.

"Remember!" Emeline called out. "The south wing cannot, I repeat, cannot be collapsed! That's where the "surviving" animals will be found!"

"Yes Ma'am!" Said DeJesus. Being tops in the demolition field and a friend of Clarence's, he knew what needed to be done.

"All of the charges are planted to collapse the building starting on the northern most section and move toward the safe zone. I've also reinforced the divider wall for added insurance."

"Thank you DeJesus. I'm just worried about my animals and not being found out."

"Once the hurricane blows through here there won't be any traces of my work." Assured DeJesus.

"All loaded and ready to go ma'am!" called one of the team.

"Excellent! Head for Tomorrow Tech! DeJesus, do your thing when the trucks meet the main road and then join me at my Jeep!" Emeline said.

The trucks rolled towards their destination and Mr. DeJesus set his timer. As he prepared to get in the Jeep, he saw headlights bouncing towards them.

"Look!" he called to Emeline. "We've got fast approaching company!"

As the charges blew, the Range Rover skidded to a stop in front of their Jeep. The driver jumped out of his vehicle and screamed, "What have you done? You've killed all of those animals!"

He lunged at Emeline and DeJesus knocked him out with a left cross to the chin. Then he grabbed the limp body and dumped him into the Rover.

"What are you doing?" Asked Emeline.

"I'm taking him and his vehicle to Mitchell. He can't stay here. He knows too much and will guess wrongly at what he doesn't know. If we leave him, he'll ruin our plans."

"Mitchell will not be happy." Frowned Emeline.

The trucks were lined up at the unloading docks at Tomorrow Tech headquarters. "B" truck and two of the "M" trucks were already unloaded when Emeline and DeJesus arrived with their "Surprise".

Clarence ran over to meet them. Emeline was courteous enough to call ahead to advise Clarence and Mitchell of the situation.

"Get him inside!" He called to DeJesus as he motioned to one of his security team. "Billy! Get this Rover in the underground garage and cover it quickly!"

He beckoned to Emeline. "Come on! Mitchell needs to see you and DeJesus so we can figure out this mess!"

"It couldn't be helped!" she said.

"Let's save the conversation until we are all together indoors." He advised. "It's getting too nasty to be standing out here."

"Alright." Said Mitchell. "Tell me what happened to get us here."

"Here" was the sub-basement conference room where they had gathered to discuss their guest who currently was tied up in the adjacent broom closet. Around the table were; Mitchell, Clarence, Emeline, DeJesus, and Jal-sa-Lem.

DeJesus filled them in on the parts they didn't know, and said, "I don't know about the rest of you, but the only thing I can think of is to dispose of him."

"Kill him?" Asked Emeline. "Just like that you would end a life? What are you?" She cried.

"I'm a man who doesn't want to lose the life he has built, that's who and what I am." Replied DeJesus.

"Easy both of you." Said Mitchell. "We aren't going to kill him, the Tacharan would not approve and neither do I. We have to find a solution that everyone can agree to."

"You are correct." Agreed Jal-sa-Lem. "Mothan II would be forever tainted."

"So, do we know who he is?" Asked DeJesus.

"I ran his plates and confirmed with his driver's license. He is Dr. Jon Schwartz. He was curator at the London Zoo for ten years until his ideas on conservation became too radical and the British Government let him go. He then joined an animal

222

rights group and has been an animal rights activist and a freedom fighter. Single, no family to speak of, no real friends around since he is always on the run. No one will find it odd that he can't be found."

"I recognize the name." Added Emeline. "He has been leaving me messages for the past month wanting to see the new building. I've just been brushing him off. I guess he decided to be more hands on."

"So, we know who and why. Now we need to answer what. As in 'what are we going to do? If we let him go, he'll ruin our project. We can't lock him up, he hasn't done anything to deserve that." Said Mitchell. "So, other plans please Clarence. You are my answer man."

"Well, I do have a rather creative idea. I agree he can't be set free. We can't kill him. The only logical solution is to take him to Mothan II."

The room sat quiet for a moment of stunned disbelief, and then Mitchell said, "You aren't kidding are you Clarence?"

"Am I laughing? Look," Clarence explained. "Dr. Schwartz is, was one of the top zoologists in the world. His passion is caring about animals. Who among the Tacharan know anything about Earths creatures? If this is presented to him correctly, this would be a dream come true for him. Totally a win-win all the way around this table."

"Well I for one would be glad to have him off Earth." Said DeJesus.

"Agreed." Confirmed Emeline. "Schwartz could destroy our careers."

Mitchell turned to Jal-sa-Lem. "What do you think my friend? After all, he will be with you and your people."

"I do like the idea of having his expertise at our disposal." Said Jal-sa-Lem. "Do you truly think he will agree?"

Mitchell answered, "Like Clarence said, he needs to be approached properly and I think Clarence is the best candidate for the job."

Jal-sa-Lem said, "Then it is agreed. Dr. Jon Schwartz, if agreeable, will become a new citizen of Mothan II in charge of Animal Welfare and Conservation."

Clarence picked up the phone from the center of the desk. "Billy, please escort our guest from the broom closet to my office. Make sure he is treated well and bring him some food. I will join you shortly. Yes, I am sure. Thank you."

"You are kidding, right?" said Jon. "Do I look like a fool to you? I must, because only a fool would believe your story."

"I said almost those exact same words when Mr. Church approached me to help him." Said Clarence. "But I can prove everything I've said to you. This is your chance to ensure the survival for these animals you love so much. You will be teaching the Tacharan scientists about earth animal care. Leading classes at their schools, providing a safe environment for these creatures."

"If, and I do mean if you are telling me the truth, this would mean everything to me. Start slowly, show me some evidence."

"I'd like to take this slowly, really I would. But we don't have that kind of time." Said Clarence. "I'm going to invite someone in to meet you, and I think this will be proof enough." Clarence picked up his phone. "Hello. Yes, we are ready for you to come in."

As Clarence put down the phone, his office door opened. Jon looked up and was grateful that he was sitting down. Jal-sa-Lem entered the room with Mitchell following him, but quite frankly Jon didn't even see Mitchell there.

Jal-sa-Lem said, "Hello Dr. Schwartz. My name is Jal-sa-Lem. I trust you are well from your encounter with Mr. DeJesus? I am very sorry for the violence."

"I..I..I'm well. Thank you." Stammered Jon. "So you are serious about me going to your planet and being in charge of your animals?"

"Very serious indeed doctor. You see, as much as we Tacharan are peaceful beings, and love animals, we do not know your animals as you do. We will all benefit by you joining us."

"This is a lot to take in." Jon said. "Can you show me this laboratory you've mentioned?"

Clarence, Jal-sa-Lem, and Jon arrived in the sub-basement laboratory a few minutes later. The process was still underway of bringing the animals from the trucks and sending them to Mothan II by way of the transportation tunnel.

"How are we proceeding?" Jal-sa-Lem asked Dr. Martinez.

She replied, "On schedule sir. We just have one more truck to unload and transport and then we have some equipment we need to send. Then you and your guests can make use of the tunnel whenever you are ready."

"Very good Patricia, thank you for all of your hard work. You are owed many thanks for your efforts."

227

"Happy to be a part of this sir."

"So as you can see Dr. Schwartz, none of the animals from the zoo were harmed in any way. They are being sent to a pure, uncontaminated world to live in peace. My people are benevolent sir. We wish for these animals to thrive just as you wish them to do." Jal-sa-Lem said.

"So, I just walk down that tunnel and like that I'm on a different planet?"

"Wherever the tunnel is programmed for, yes. You certainly don't want to end up at the bottom of Loch Ness!"

"Ok, I think I'm in. What about my stuff? My apartment?"

"I will make all the arraignments to collect your belongings and send them to you." Assured Clarence.

Jal-sa-Lem said, "I shall go through with you Jon so that I can make introductions for you."

"Thank you." Said Dr. Schwartz. "I appreciate that. This still doesn't seem real."

As he and Jal-sa-Lem walked into the tunnel, Dr. Schwartz called back over his shoulder, "Hey Clarence! Don't forget my bike!" And then he vanished.

CHAPTER TWENTY-ONE

MOTHAN II – CAPITAL CITY: ALBA

Earth calendar: November 6th, 2021

Mothan II calendar: Aon 1, 1000

"On this day, one revolution around our new sun, life began on this dead planet. That life gave the Tacharan our new hope for a fresh start, a life of peace. I am pleased to dedicate this Garden of Tranquility and Remembrance for those we lost on Mothan I and for those whose hard work, dedication, and sacrifice helped to create this new world for us." Cre-na-Tal rang the ceremonial bells as she stepped aside from the entrance to the gardens. The audience applauded. "The council has also decreed that our calendar would begin again on this day, a true new beginning for our new world. Please enjoy the gardens and refreshments."

Mitchell turned to Jon and said, "So doctor. What do you think?"

"This has been an amazing dream come true." Dr. Schwartz said. "I truly feel fulfillment here and a peace I've only dreamt of."

"I'm glad to hear that." said Mitchell.

Cre-na-tal walked up to Mitchell and said, "I am so happy to see you again my friend."

"Likewise." Replied Mitchell. "I must say, you look wonderful! This new world seems to have had a positive effect on you."

"More than you realize. My cells have almost completely regenerated, and my longevity prognoses is promising." She smiled. "It may be an effect of the terraforming process, the new atmosphere, the foods and water, we aren't sure. I was walking on Mothan II while the terraforming process was still underway, so that also may be an influence on my renewed health. Whatever the cause, I feel better than I have in quite some time."

"Amazing! I couldn't be happier." Said Mitchell.

231

"Mitchell, may I have a word in private with you?" Asked Cre-na-Tal.

"Of course.   Dr. Schwartz, would you mind excusing us please?"

"Not at all!   Some of the young ones have questions about the newest avian species we've introduced here.   I'm always happy to be teaching!" Jon said as he hurried away.

"So, what's so important?" Asked Mitchell.

"We need to discuss the future. Specifically, do we share the terraforming technology with the Raiders? Kem-ka-Jen says no but I, and several others, do not agree with him. If the Síocháin, as the Raiders were once known, could have a home its possible they would return to their lives of peace."

"And it's just as possible that they will abuse and destroy their new home just as they did their first planet."

"True, however, it is not our place to project onto them what they might do wrong.   It is our responsibility to help those we can with the resources we have."

Mitchell shook his head. "I don't know about this. I'm going to need to think on it. In the past 400 plus years on Earth, I've seen many good things done for some, but I've also seen the best intentions lead to ruin for others. I'd like to think you are correct. The Raiders would settle down and go back to being peaceful, but it's very hard to change minds and behaviors that have been in place for so long."

"It would be helpful if we knew if there were any sympathizers within the raider's numbers." Thought Cre-na-Tal out loud.

"Can we infiltrate them?" Asked Mitchell. "Do they look like the Tacharan?"

Cre-na-Tal laughed. "Actually Mitchell, they look like humans! There are slight variances in the ears and forehead, but nothing that couldn't be taken care of with a little cosmetic alteration. Remember too, they have spent the last 1000 years fighting for everything. They are fierce and fight amongst themselves for sport. Whomever we choose needs to be able to handle their own in a brawl."

Mitchell nodded his head. "I have a couple of candidates in mind."

TOMORROW TECH INC.
HEADQUARTERS

Billy and DeJesus sat in Mitchell's office listening to the plan.

"You two are the best bet for this being a successful mission. With your military background and covert-ops experience, I know you will succeed."

Billy asked, "So to make sure I get it right, you are going to change our faces to look like the Raiders, get us on to one of their ships, and then we need to find some of their people who want to make peace with the galaxy? Anything else while we are there?"

"Sounds like a walk in the park sir. When do we go?" Asked DeJesus.

"Cre-na-Tal and her people are still making arraignments for your transportation. Getting you on a raider ship will be the hardest part, but a couple of her people are figuring that one out. A Tacharan surgeon will be joining us here to complete the facial transformation and help us fabricate raider clothing. Luckily they don't subscribe to any formal uniforms, so that part will be quite easy. The other obstacle is that we can't do anything on Mothan II. There are too many opponents to this plan including the chief elder."

"So," asked DeJesus, "the plan is to hope all goes well and ask forgiveness later?"

"It's either this, or Cre-na-Tal confronts Kem-ka-Jen in front of everyone and let majority rule. I'm advocating a middle ground approach. You two go in, find allies, and then we open the discussion up to all the Tacharan. That way we have more leverage against the chief elder and his supporters."

"I agree with you." Said Billy. "We will find your supporters in the raider's ranks and come back with the Intel you need."

"Cre-na-Tal and her friends only worry is that the Raiders won't take to the proposal and either execute you or try to locate Mothan II. We can't let either happen." Explained Mitchell.

"Don't worry sir. They won't know who we are or where we are from until we are sure of their commitment." Said Billy.

"Good, make it happen gentlemen!" said Mitchell.

"Good lord you are one ugly mess!" joked Billy as he looked upon DeJesus' new face. His earlobes had been extended and now rested on his collarbone. Running horizontally across his forehead was a cluster of ridges resembling a mountain range as seen from a distance. The "range" ran from temple to temple.

"Really now?" Asked DeJesus. "Have you held a mirror lately?"

Billy turned around and stared at himself in the mirror on the wall behind him. "Wow! I'm just as bad as you!" He said with a laugh.

237

"This isn't a beauty contest gentlemen." Said Clarence. "I'm just grateful to Doctor All-da-Tan for coming here to do this for us. As of today, DeJesus your name is BeTok and Billy, you are KenTal. Learn them, use them. Don't get caught using your earth names."

All-da-Tan replied, "Not for you alone. I am hoping for this to be a successful mission and one day for the Síocháin to live in peace with the galaxy and themselves. Only then will I feel that the Tacharan are truly freed from what has happened."

"This is going to happen doc." Promised Billy. "We aint gonna let you down, no Sir!"

DeJesus nodded his agreement. "Yeah, what he said. We don't fail in our missions. That's why we are still around."

"Thank you gentlemen. I appreciate your resolve. I will see you when you return so that I can reverse the surgery I've performed today."

CHAPTER TWENTY-TWO

Earth Year 2022

Somewhere near the Zelad star system

on the Planet Kadiliman

Due to the toxic atmosphere on Kadiliman, BeTok and KenTal, along with the other Raiders, wore their air breathers which covered the majority of their faces.

The Raiders had already completed their air attacks and were finishing up their ground assault when Jal-sa-Lem had landed his scout ship in a secluded canyon close to the ground troops.

"Quickly now!" He said. "Get your air breathers on and blend in with one of the Raider squads. With your faces covered, no one will know you aren't part of the original landing party."

"Don't they know how to count?" Asked BeTok.

"In a Raider ground assault, it's all boots on the ground. They aren't concerned with a lot of order and precision." Explained Jal-sa-Lem. "Hurry now so you don't miss the ship! Contact us as soon as you can."

"Roger that." Said KenTal as he and BeTok exited the scout ship.

Jal-sa-Lem quickly lifted off from the planet's surface and headed away from the Raider attack. Getting caught by them was not in the plan. As he flew away, he wondered if he would see them again.

The frigid air was damp and biting. Billy could feel it deep in his bones and it made him ache from head to toe.

At first the cold aboard the ship felt good coming from the harsh steaming hot planet. But as Billy and DeJesus made their way into the ships dark and musty interior, the temperature became unbearable.

"How do these raiders handle this?" Asked Billy. "I feel as if I'm going to freeze to death."

"We will acclimate." Answered DeJesus. "The conditions on this ship are obviously due to resource shortages. I'm more concerned about the food and water supply here. I can always put on another coat, but I'm not going to eat that coat!"

"Hopefully we can complete our mission quickly and get home!" said Billy. "Get us out of here before I turn into a popsicle and your first steak dinner is on me."

"You're on bud." Agreed DeJesus.

They had boarded the **Quemado**, a Raider troop transport ship twenty minutes earlier along with the ground troops. Once aboard they quickly separated themselves from the other troopers and hid in what appeared to be a storage/supply room.

The plan was to stay as inconspicuous as possible until the transport met up with the fleet. There they would make their way to one of the main housing ships and start their search for supporters of their mission.

"Before I get that steak though, we need to find a place to hole up until we reach the fleet." Said DeJesus. "The more we wander around the more likely someone is to question us."

Billy nodded. "Jal-sa-Lem said that everything is rationed so we might have difficulty with getting any food or water until we find help."

"Good thing we brought some rations, but they won't last long. If this storage room isn't visited often, it should work for us to stay here. The fleet is only two days away from what I heard on the transport."

"Alright." Agreed Billy. I'll see what's in here that we can use while you contact Jal-sa-Lem and let him know we made it."

"Sounds good." Replied DeJesus. Rolling up his sleeve, he accessed the sub-dermal transmitter in his forearm and tapped out the signal agreed upon for 'safe landing'.

Time crawled while they waited to meet up with the fleet. DeJesus snuck out a couple times to gather some warmer clothing and anything he could find that resembled food. Returning this last time, he found Billy curled up and asleep in a corner.

"Wake up!" DeJesus said. "You need to be alert when I'm out of the room! Do you want to get caught?"

"Come on!" It's been almost two days. No one's come down here and we are about to join the fleet. Give me a break. I'm frozen, hungry, and overall not in a good mood so back off!"

"I get it, believe me, but our mission is too important to be slacking." DeJesus said. "Let's get ready to jump ship. I found where the ground troops exit."

"Alright. Sorry." Said Billy.

"No issue." DeJesus shook his head. "I get it."

Grabbing their gear, they made their way down two decks and to the ships rear. There they found some troopers starting to assemble.

"Move over to the far corner." Said DeJesus. "Limit eye contact also." He warned.

As they made their way across the staging area, a large Raider backed into Billy nearly knocking him down.

Already tense, Billy said, "Watch it!"

Turning around, the Raider squared off with Billy. Standing a good ten inches taller than Billy, he looked like a mountain.

"Apologize to me or die." The Raider snarled.

"Apologize for what? The fact that you can't walk a straight line? Leave me alone pal!" Replied Billy.

The Raider balled up his fist and drew back to strike as DeJesus got between them.

"Hey now! Let's slow down!" DeJesus said. "We are all wound up from the raid and need to relax. Tell you what friend, let us buy you a drink when we get back to the habitation ship. How's that sound?"

"Ugh, yeah, whatever. Just stay out of my way."
The raider sneered and wandered off.

"Billy, seriously. What part of inconspicuous
don't you comprehend?" DeJesus whispered.

"Not my fault!" Billy deflected. "He ran into me!"

"Look man, I'm not getting killed because you got
your feelings hurt, got it?" DeJesus said jabbing
his finger at Billy.

"Yeah, yeah I got it." Replied Billy.

"Good. Now sit down and keep out of trouble."
Ordered DeJesus.

A quiet hour later, the ship wide bells sounded
informing everyone that an announcement was
coming. The assembled troops had grown in
numbers, and eagerly looked towards the speakers.

"All troopers report to staging and unloading." The
ships computer said. "Docking with Habitation
Ship II in ten minutes."

A cheer went around the room while other
moaned. DeJesus and Billy smiled.

Billy said, "I guess we are from Habitation Ship II."

"Remember," DeJesus said, "Stay close to me. We need to move fast and get out of sight."

"Roger that." Replied Billy. "I'm just hoping the next ship is warmer."

A loud metallic clang rang through the room as the two ships reunited. With a hiss of equalizing pressure, the large access hatch rolled away. The eager crowd pushed their way towards the exit. DeJesus, suddenly fearing a check-in process, restrained Billy from joining them.

"Not so fast, let them push their way over there. I want to see how they are greeted."

As the two slowly moved towards the opening, they watched the first group move from the transport to the habitation ship.

They walked through an arch and were bombarded with an intense blue light.

It lasted just a moment and then the troopers scattered through what appeared to be a reception center. Some were greeted by those waiting in the room, others made a beeline out of the area and disappeared through various opening around the room.

"What's the blue light for?" Asked Billy.

"I'm thinking decontaminating us so we don't bring any disease from the planet." Answered DeJesus. "I'm just glad there's not a check-in process. Our intel didn't go this far."

"Lucky us! We're ground breakers!" Joked Billy. "Let's move!"

They walked down the ramp and through the blue light. It tingled but didn't hurt. They then moved across the room to the closest exit.

Exiting the reception area, they found themselves in what could only be described as a market. 'Street' vendors were everywhere calling for buyers to check out their wares. Music was coming from competing artists trying to draw attention to their corner of the huge space. Then the food smells hit them and their mouths watered as their stomachs rumbled.

"Food!" Said Billy. "Real food. I'm so hungry I don't care what it's made from."

"Control yourself buddy. We'll eat. I'm watching them. It seems to be a barter system. You see that big Raider? He just traded his gloves for a platter of food. We can save the jewels and gold that Jal-sa-Lem gave us for later. All these extra clothes I scavenged are going to be our currency!"

Billy smiled. "It is warmer on this ship. Let's get in there!"

They moved forward and their senses were almost overpowered by the sights, smells, and sounds. As they neared the first food stall, Billy took off an outer cloak and offered it to the woman frying something unidentifiable. She grinned at him, took the garment to examine. Satisfied, she scooped up a large portion of the delicious smelling whatever and handed it to Billy. He smiled and nodded his thanks as he took the food.

Suddenly hesitant, Billy offered the plate to DeJesus and said, "Would you like some?"

DeJesus chuckled. "Naw, that's alright. You first. After all it was your jacket."

Billy smiled weakly as he looked at the food, but the smell and his hunger won out as he picked up a piece and popped it into his mouth. As he chewed his eyes lit up.

"This is freaking awesome!" He exclaimed. "Really, give it a try!" He insisted.

DeJesus was hungry so he reached over and took a piece as well.

"You're right Billy. Whatever it is, it's good!"

Temporarily forgetting the 'lay-low' plan, the duo wandered around the market eating and looking at the curiosities from a thousand worlds the Raiders had claimed.

"I wonder if anything here is from Mothan." Pondered Billy. "If so, I'd love to bring something back for Cre-na-Tal."

"That would be cool," agreed DeJesus, "But not our mission. Look over there. It seems to be a bar. Maybe we can eavesdrop on the crowd to get our bearings."

As they focused on crossing the market to get to the bar, they failed to notice the hooded figure following them.

Claiming a dark corner in the bar, DeJesus and Billy surveyed the crowd.

Billy said, "Ya know, no matter where I went back home, bars were always the same. Same sticky floor, same sweaty smells, same hard chairs. How do they do it?" He asked amused.

"And where exactly is 'back home' stranger?"

They looked up as the cloaked figure sat across from them. From his hand placement they both were confident that their new acquaintance was armed.

DeJesus said, "Hello friend. What can we do for ya?"

250

"You can start by telling me who you are and where you're from."

Billy chuckled nervously. "What do you mean? We are all from here, right? I mean come on. I was just referring to the habitation ship I was raised on."

"And which one would that be?" Asked their tablemate.

"Ship number four." Billy said.

"Ah! Ship four! Yes, a good one!" The stranger replied. "Tell ya what, we got off on the wrong foot. I want to buy us all a round." With that, he signaled to the bartender for three drinks.

"That isn't necessary." Said DeJesus. "No hard feelings. We need to be moving on." He and Billy began to rise when they heard the electronic whine coming from under the table.

"I would suggest," said their host, "That you sit back down. This Tazze pistol has a very sensitive trigger."

Billy and DeJesus looked at each other and sat down as the bartender delivered their drinks.

"I must say, your disguises are quite good. You had me fooled until you started speaking." Looking at Billy he said, "You in particular have a very unique accent. I've never heard anything quite like it. Now you see that doorway to your left? We are all going to get up, take our drinks, and make our way over there. Try anything and I'll stun you both and turn you over to the authorities. You'll be instantly found guilty of spying and executed. Do as I say and you may live an extra day or two. Now, let's go."

All three stood and moved. The bartender intercepted them and opened the door. Inside was a cramped and disorganized office. A ratty couch lined one wall and faced a beat up wooden desk piled high with papers.

"Sit on the couch." They were ordered as the bartender stepped into the room with them. He closed the door, crossed his arms, and leaned backwards against the only exit from the room.

The stranger sat down into the only chair in the room, a black leather high back behind the desk.

"Alright." He said. "Let's begin with something easy. Tell me your names and where you are from."

DeJesus said, "My name is BeTok and this is KenTal. We are ground troops originally from Habitation Ship Four recently transferred here."

The room filled with the whine from the Tazze pistol and this time it was visibly pointing directly at them.

"Ok. I understand. You were given names and a cover story to use. I know the game. What I need to figure out is, why are you here? Once I know that, I'll know how to proceed."

Everyone sat in silence for a minute. The bartender growled and said, "Boss, just shoot them and let me dump them in an airlock. They aren't Raider or Siochain so they are enemies."

The 'boss' held up his free hand and said, "there may be a third option here. Let's try this. I'll go first. My name is CadaRon. I was once the captain of one of our finest battle cruisers, but I tired of the constant destruction. So now I'm retired from the military and spend my days looking for solutions to our current life. Something about you encourages me, so tell me something believable before I need to let my friend here blow you out into space.

DeJesus looked at Billy and shrugged. Billy said, "We are here to make contact. Looks like we did."

"Okay. Good or bad, here goes. What I can tell you is this. My name is DeJesus and this is Billy. We come from a planet your people haven't found yet and I'm hoping you never do. We're friends with what's left of a race you tried to exterminate.

"So." Said CadaRon. "Are you here to avenge your friends or to stop us before we find your planet?"

"Neither." Said Billy. "We fixed them up with a new planet and some of them thought we could do the same for ya'll so you can stop destroying others' homes." Billy turned towards the bartender. "I recognize the name you said 'Siochain'. It means 'peaceful ones'. Dontcha want to be them again instead of the Raiders?"

CadaRon sighed heavily, "I was born a Raider. I was a Raider captain. My ship and crew destroyed dozens of planets and countless lives. I've renounced that and now I am Siochain. There is a growing movement among our people to end the raiding but we don't know how to survive otherwise. Tell me, what are the people you have met and helped?"

DeJesus shook his head. "No. I'm not giving you that. Our mission was to make contact with anyone sympathetic to our plan and set up a line of communication. Details come with trust and we aren't there yet."

"Understandable." Said CadaRon. "Trust must be earned. So how do you propose we build on our new-found relationship?"

"We brought you non-trackable communicators. You and our friends will work out a timetable to talk, meet, and eventually secure a new world for your people. In the meantime, you should start looking for a system where you want your new home."

"But a planet that will sustain us will more than likely be inhabited. You are still talking about wiping out a race to take their home. The Siochain will not do that again." Swore CadaRon.

DeJesus and Billy smiled. Billy said, "Oh have we got a surprise for you! But first, do you have something to eat?"

MOTHAN II

"Shouldn't we have had another contact by now?"
Said McDougal. "It's been days since they
signaled that they made it."

Jal-sa-Lem thought (Patience McDougal. They
have not sent a trouble signal so we still have hope
for a fruitful outcome. It could take them weeks to
find a sympathetic ear.)

McDougal sighed, (I know you are correct my
friend. I just don't like the waiting!)

(Understandable. I too wonder about their safety.)

Just then the console on Jal-sa-Lems work station
lit up.

(Incoming signal!) He thought to McDougal.

(Is it from our team?) McDougal replied.

Jal-sa-Lem paused a moment before answering.
(Yes! Yes, it is! It is the pre-arraigned signal for
safe and contact made.)

257

(Cre-na-Tal must know of this.) Replied McDougal.

(I'm here.) Responded Cre-na-Tal. (The signal was routed to my console as well. This is most welcomed news!)

(Now.) Thought Jal-sa-Lem. (We wait for the rendezvous signal and I'll retrieve them.)

(Wonderful, more waiting.) Thought McDougal.

RAIDER FLEET

Habitation Ship II

One week later

CadaRon said, "It's still remarkable that you've created a new world from a dead one."

DeJesus replied, "You've seen the video evidence. I'd explain the science to you, but that's not my area."

"It still seems like a miracle to me." Said Billy. "If I hadn't seen it and been there, I'd be skeptical too."

CadaRon replied, "One of our scientists tell me that this was pondered long ago when our planet was failing, but our science wasn't advanced enough. Maybe if we had tried harder, instead of destroying worlds we would have learned to create a new one."

"No sense dwelling on that. Have you located a suitable system to settle?" Asked Billy.

"Yes, actually we have. The Cirsis System. It has a star similar to our former home and there is a dead planet the right distance for our temperature needs."

"I gotta ask," said DeJesus, "This wasn't a planet you wiped out, right?"

"No!" CadaRon said. "That was a stipulation I insisted upon when I asked my team to find us a planet. I don't think I could live there otherwise."

"Okay, good." Said DeJesus. "That would just be wrong. Give me the coordinates for the planet along with the DNA samples we discussed."

"My team is preparing everything for you. They should be ready by days end. What else do you require?" Asked CadaRon.

"We will need transport away from your fleet so our people can retrieve us." Said DeJesus.

"I will take you myself. Very few still have access to use a scout ship, but I have many friends." Assured CadaRon.

The next day, CadaRon, DeJesus, and Billy made their way to the space docks. CadaRon greeted the officer in charge.

"Major Remchar! How are you? How is your father Captain KemChar hmm? Taking good care of my cruiser I hope?" He chuckled.

"Hello sir, good to see you!" Replied RemChar. "I'm well, father is good too. Thank you again for recommending me for this promotion. I truly appreciate it."

"Ah you deserved it." Said CadaRon. "Besides those officer tags look perfect on you!"

"Well thank you again sir. What can I do for you today?" RemChar asked.

"I'm working with these two ground troopers. I see potential in them like I see with you." (Remchar beamed at the compliment.) "I want to take them out in a scout ship, show them what it takes to be a pilot for the cause."

"Yes sir, sounds great. I'm sure you'd be the best instructor anyone could hope for." Said RemChar. "I just need your flight clearance and fuel consumption allowances waiver."

CadaRon moved closer to RemChar and put his hand on RemChar's shoulder covering his Majors' tags.

"Son remember who I am and what I've done for you, your father, for the whole damn fleet. And now this? I do this for our people's future. I'm not going for a joy ride! This literally could be what ensures our survival and you want papers from me?!"

"I'm..I'm sorry Sir! I wasn't thinking. Please forgive me." Stammered RemChar.

He turned towards his console and quickly punched in a series of commands.

"Your ship is on track K-9 sir, ready for you to depart." Said RemChar.

"Thank you son. We'll be back soon." Said CadaRon. Motioning to DeJesus and Billy, CadaRon quickly walked over to the waiting ship.

The three climbed the entry ramp and buckled in. CadaRon taxied to the airlock and when the signal was given, launched them out of the ship.

As they flew away from the fleet, CadaRon asked, "So are you going to give me coordinates or do you want me to just fly around a bit?"

"You are sure we aren't being followed CadaRon?" Asked DeJesus.

"Nothing on scanners, nothing visual. I'm pretty sure we aren't being tracked by anyone." Said CadaRon.

DeJesus said, "Okay then. Here are the coordinates we need to go to."

CadaRon looked at their destination and his blood chilled. "Why was this location chosen? Is this a cruel joke you're playing on me? If so, I don't find it very funny."

"No joke." Said DeJesus. "There is some ancient tech buried there we discovered. We are going to use that to get home."

CadaRon explained. "This was the Tacharan home world and the last mission I took part in. The Tacharan are the reason I am no longer a Raider. Many generations ago, our races were friends, and now we have destroyed them."

"Maybe by leading your people to their new home and stopping the genocide, you can find some peace." Said Billy.

"Maybe." Said CadaRon. "Maybe."

They circle Mothan in silence. It took all of Billy's willpower not to scream at CadaRon for the destruction below. For his part, CadaRon's chest felt heavy reliving the events of his last visit to this planet.

"Coordinates below, but I don't see anything." Said CadaRon.

"We need to land. There are some underground caverns where we will find the equipment we need." Said Billy.

CadaRon put the ship down and opened the hatch. Turning to DeJesus and Billy he said, "I want to tell you both, no matter if this all works out or not, I appreciate you risking everything to come to my people. I vow that one way or another, we will end the raiding."

Billy said, "That's good, but also promise me that after the Raiders are gone and the Siochain are restored, you won't let your people forget what has happened. History forgotten is bound to be history repeated. Don't let your people repeat their mistakes."

"I swear to you I won't let that happen." Promised CadaRon.

Billy and DeJesus put their breathers on, exited the ship and waved as CadaRon departed. They waited a moment until he was completely out of view and then turned towards the mountain range and began walking. As they neared the rock wall, an opening came into view.

"That must be for us." Said Billy. "Let's go home!"

They entered the cavern and paused a moment to let their eyes adjust to the dim light. Moving forward through the deserted sanctuary they marveled that the Tacharan had survived so long down here.

Just then, they heard noise ahead of them.

"Whose there?" Asked Billy.

"Billy? DeJesus? It is Jal-sa-Lem."

They all stepped out into the open and came together for handshakes.

"It is so good to see you again my friends." Said Jal-sa-Lem. "I am relieved that you are safe."

"I'm not kidding, it was a little iffy in the beginning, but I have great hopes for this working out." Said DeJesus.

266

"Can we go home now?" Asked Billy. "I really need a burger and fries!"

DeJesus laughed and said, "That sounds good, but don't forget you owe me a steak dinner!"

"Come this way my friends. The transportation tunnel has one last journey to make. I've set the controls for Tomorrow Tech headquarters and I know that there are some anxious people waiting to see you." Said Jal-sa-Lem.

They headed deeper into the cavern until they came to the transportation tunnel. Jal-sa-Lem instructed them to stand near the entrance while he initiated the transfer.

"Once I hit the send switch I'll join you and we will go through together. After we have returned to Earth, I am going to create a feedback loop that will overload the system and destroy this tunnel and terminal." Jal-sa-Lem explained.

"Why do you want to do that? Asked Billy.

"Just in case your new friend CadaRon isn't as convincing as he hopes, we don't want the Raiders to find this tunnel and try to follow us to Earth or find Mothan II. Besides, there isn't anything left here for my people. Our home is Mothan II." Said Jal-sa-Lem. "Come my friends, let's go."

CHAPTER TWENTY-THREE

Raider Fleet

CadaRon docked his ship and as quickly as possible, made his way to leave the landing bay.

As he reached the exit, he heard, "Captain CadaRon! Sir, a moment of your time."

He turned and saw RemChar quickly approaching him.

"Yes major. I am pressed for time, but what can I do for you?"

"Thank you, sir. There is someone here to see you. But also, what happened to your two troopers? I didn't see them return with you." Said RemChar.

"Oh, I dismissed them as soon as we landed. I don't hold out any promise for either of them. I was mistaken about their commitment to the cause." Replied CadaRon.

"And exactly what 'cause' it that CadaRon?"

CadaRon turned around recognizing the voice behind him.

"Captain KemChar! What a pleasant surprise! What brings you to our ship?" Asked CadaRon.

"I was speaking to my son earlier and he relayed your greetings to me. I had spare time and thought I would come see my son and former captain." Answered KemChar.

"Excellent!" Said CadaRon. "We need to have a drink later before you return to your ship."

"Actually, let's do that now." Said KemChar. "I have some questions for you regarding this little trip you just took and your recent activities. There are some in command that are questioning your commitment to our people."

"My commitment!? Are you serious? I have dedicated my life to our people! How dare I be questioned about commitment?" exclaimed CadaRon.

"It is because of your record that I requested the opportunity to speak with you. If it were anyone but you, you would be answering these questions in front of the full council." Explained KemChar.

CadaRon squared his shoulders and said, "Fine old friend. Let us go to my quarters and have that drink. Then I will answer all of your questions and hopefully put the question of my loyalty to rest."

TOMORROW TECH

Two Weeks Later

Jal-sa-Lem entered Mitchell's office with Cre-na-Tal.

"Still nothing?" Asked Mitchell.

"No. No contact with CadaRon at all. He's missed every arranged time. We fear that he has been found out, and knowing the Raider mindset, executed." Said Cre-na-Tal.

"There is still hope that the communication relays aren't functioning properly, or some other interference is involved. If he was discovered, he may have needed to flee and doesn't have the equipment we left him. Without evidence, I prefer to believe that all is not lost." Said Jal-sa-Lem.

"So, what do you propose?" Asked Mitchell.

Cre-na-Tal said, "Could we send our team back in to search for him?"

"No too risky." Said Mitchell. "I'm not willing to risk our people on a possible suicide mission."

"Begging your pardon sir, and no disrespect meant, but you already did once. What's one more try?" Asked DeJesus entering the office with Billy.

"Yes sir. We are ready whenever you give the greenlight." Agreed Billy.

"No gentlemen. Last time was dangerous. If CadaRon has been discovered, it would be foolishness to return to the Raider fleet. Work on establishing communications or come up with another plan, but without contact from CadaRon, we aren't going there again." Declared Mitchell. "He's on his own."

EPILOGUE

Earth Year 2025

Main Conference Room at T.T.I.

The conference room was packed with reporters and dignitaries from around the globe. The word had gone out that Mitchell Church would be making a huge announcement about the future of his company and a new discovery. No news outlet in the world wanted to be left out.

As Mitchell approached the podium, the crowd came to their feet and began applauding.

Mitchell raised his hands to silence the crowd and said, "Please everyone. Have a seat." And they complied.

"Thank you all for coming out today. First, I would like to announce that I am stepping down from all my official capacities here at Tomorrow Tech and turning over ownership and control to my most trusted friend, Clarence Baldwin." Mitchell announced.

At this the crowd of reporters jumped to their feet and began yelling questions.

Mitchell again raised his hands and said, "Please take your seats and quiet down. After my announcements you will have time for questions."

The crowd continued to murmur amongst themselves but did settle down somewhat.

"Now, since the transfer of ownership is already complete, I want to thank Clarence for allowing me to use his facilities for this press conference." Mitchell said as he looked at Clarence and smiled.

Clarence called out, "You are always welcomed here sir."

"Thank you." Replied Mitchell. "Now then, everyone settle back and get comfortable. I have quite a story to tell you. My next announcement is that I will be going away for a long time. You see, today March 8th 2025, you know me as Mitchell Church, but that is not my true name. My birth name is McDougal of Inverness, I was born in the year of our Lord 1541 and this is my story.......

List of Main Characters

<u>Earthlings:</u>

<u>McDougal of Inverness, Scotland</u>

Aliases:

<u>Douglas of Errogie, Scotland</u>

<u>Robert Mitchell – Canada</u>

<u>Mitchell Church - Houston, Texas</u>

<u>Clarence Baldwin:</u> Assistant to Mitchell Church

<u>Rosalind Frasier: Inverness, Scotland</u>

<u>Brian Edgars: Dunedin, New Zealand</u>

<u>Michael Andrews:</u> Boat Captain – Nessie Tours

Ian Daniels: Chief Constable Fort Augustus Police Department

Patricia Martinez: Chief Scientist at T.T.I.

Simon Van den Berg: Editor in Chief, De Gelderlander

Maarten Jansen: De Gelderlander reporter

Dr. Alexandra De Vries: Professor of Aquatic Biology at Utrecht University, Netherlands

Tacharan:

Name structure

1st section, three letters, given name

2nd section, two letters, place in society

> ka = Leadership
>
> sa = Space Services
>
> da = Sciences
>
> na = Education
>
> wa = Civil Defense

3rd section, three letters, family surname

Kem-ka-Jen: Chief Elder

Mar-wa-Len: Guardian

Jal-sa-Lem: Scout and first Tacharan to contact an Earthling

Jol-sa-Pel: First Tacharan to study Earth

Mak-na-Tal: Educator

Cre-na-Tal: Educator

All-da-Tan: Physician

Raiders (Síocháin):

<u>SlayThan</u>: Captain of the Raider Battle Cruiser Lagartheria

<u>KaMal</u>: Science Officer aboard the Lagartheria

<u>Ry-Lei</u>: the Lagartherias helmsman

<u>RanGelian</u>: Supreme Commander of the Raider military

<u>CadaRon</u>: Captain of the Raider Battle Cruiser Tolowar

<u>KemChar</u>: 1st Officer aboard the Tolowar

Gaelic to English Translations

Tacharan: Changeling

Adhar: Sky

Inneal: Machine

Allmhara: Alien, foreign, strange

Slainte Mhath: Good Health

Síocháin: Peace

Mar Sin Leat: Good-bye

Mothan: Giant

Seanair: Grandfather

The Parting Glass

The tune appears as early as the 1600s - in the Skene Manuscript, a collection of Scottish airs written at various dates between 1615 and 1635, and in the Guthrie Manuscript (c 1675 - Edinburgh University Library). It is also in Playford's Original Scots Tunes (1700).
Before Auld Lange Syne, this song was the most popular parting song in Scotland. It was printed on broadsides as early as 1770 and saw a resurgence of popularity in the late 1800s. Several copies of these broadsides can be found at the Bodleian Library.

It first appears in book form in the Scots Musical Museum (1803/4). It then appears in Scots Songs by Herd (1869).

It was known in part at least as early as 1605, when a portion of the first tanza was written in a farewell letter, as a poem now known as "Armstrong's Goodnight", by one of the Border Reivers executed that year for the murder in 1600 of Sir John Carmichael, Warden of the Scottish West March. [recorded in George MacDonald Fraser, Steel Bonnets: The Story of the Anglo-Scottish Border Reivers, Harper Collins: London, 1995, ppg. 140-143].

Neil Gow, the celebrated Scottish fiddler, published a version of the tune as "Goodnight and Joy Be Wi' Ye A'" in the late 18th century, with the comment: "This tune is played at the conclusion of every convivial dancing meeting throughout Scotland."

The song is also known as Good Night and Joy Be With You All.

Many thanks to clans.org for this information. Learn more about Scottish clans at:

http://www.clans.org.uk/partglass.html